To Roy best wishes Chas

THE

SAME

TREE

Chas Gould

Chapter 1

Life and Death

Aleppo 16th October 2016

The room was completely dark with no light penetrating the boarded-up windows, but he knew instinctively that now was the time. He edged his way across the debris strewn floor until he reached Stevie's body covered in old sacks.

"Wake up, Stevie, wake up, it's time."

Stevie failed to stir immediately so Chris shook her violently.

"Come on Stevie, wake up. It's time to go."

"Go where?" replied Stevie as she began to surface.

"Home" said Chris.

Then they heard the outer door being opened followed by footsteps coming down the corridor towards their cell.

"Stevie, listen, we are being taken away from here. It is important that you do not say anything or look at anyone. Keep your eyes down and look only at the floor. If you look up and make eye-contact with anyone it could get us killed."

Just then the footsteps stopped outside their cell and the door was unlocked and opened. The light from a single bulb in the corridor shone into their cell and Chris could see the boarded-up windows and the corner of the room piled with faeces that he and Stevie had been forced to use as a toilet. Whatever happened next Chris was going to be happy to be out of that room.

There was a low command in Arabic and Chris whispered to Stevie.

"They want us to go with them."

Stevie and Chris did as they were instructed, only to receive brutal jabs from the barrel of an AK47 for their compliance. Keeping their heads down they were led through a maze of corridors and rubble strewn courtyards. Eventually they came to the old walls of the city which stood like the teeth of an old man, more gaps than wall. Their captors became nervous at this point and pushed Chris and Stevie through one of these gaps first and then, when nothing happened, they followed quietly themselves. An hour later the group stopped on the edge of a large patch of open flat farmland. There they waited silently, Chris, Stevie and the three fighters from the Al-Nusra Front. After a while there came the sound of an approaching helicopter which soon appeared flying low towards them. It was now getting light, and Chris risked lifting his head and saw that the helicopter was completely devoid of any markings. It landed on the far side of the open ground and instantly, as the wheels touched the ground, the side door slid open. Two hooded men dressed entirely in black jumped down and pointed their guns towards the waiting group. When they had assessed it was safe one of them barked out a command and into the open doorway stepped a middle-aged man with a wild and unruly black beard. Even from that distance Chris could see that he stood defiantly with an air of injured pride. He jumped down and stood between the two hooded men and now in the doorway stood a third hooded man in black with an automatic pistol pointed at the back of the bearded man's head. Chris and Stevie were then pushed forward in the direction of the helicopter and gestured to keep walking. At the same time the bearded man started walking towards them. As Chris and Stevie passed by him, they could see the intense anger in his eyes, and it was directed towards them. Chris and Stevie reached the helicopter the same time that he reached their captors who started hugging the bearded man.

"Quickly" barked one of the hooded men.

"Get in the bird. We need to get out of here!" Stevie climbed up into the helicopter but as Chris started to clamber aboard there was a loud cry behind him and he turned to see the bearded man pointing at the helicopter and venting his anger in a string of expletives.

"Quick, get in now" shouted the hooded man as he started to shut the helicopter door. At this point the Al-Nusra fighters started firing at the helicopter. Stevie scrambled into the back of the helicopter and Chris threw himself aboard. The door was nearly closed, and Chris turned to see the bearded man shaking his fists at him. As he did so, Chris took a bullet in the throat which passed through his neck and severed his spinal cord killing him instantly.

Washington - 3 Months Later

Stevie looked across at her father, the US Secretary of State. Their relationship had improved greatly since Stevie's rescue. George McMaster, her father, had been forced during Stevie's capture to face his inadequacies as a father. He had acknowledged his previous distance and lack of affection for his daughter. Equally, Stevie had come to see her father through softer eyes. Stevie for her part now accepted that her father had always loved her even if he had failed to show it. Also, she could now accept that she had been unfair to have blamed him entirely for the deterioration in their relationship.

The Secretary of State leant forward in his large leather chair closing the distance between him and his daughter.

"Stevie, are you sure this is what you want to do?

Stevie smiled back at her father.

"Yes Dad, believe me it is different this time. Before, I was running away. I wanted to defy you. I had graduated and needed you to realise that I could make my own choices. All I remember of that time is that we were both very angry with each other. You said that I only ever thought of myself and never did anything for anyone else. I wanted to show you that you were wrong. I chose to do it in way that would cause you the maximum discomfort. If Mum had been around things might been different. The thing is, the time spent in captivity changed me. The death of the Swedish boy along with my discussions with Chris caused me to reflect on my stupid behaviour. Though I did not know him for long, Chris had a big impact on me. In the hours together I learnt so much from him. He died saving me and I feel I must pick up from where he left off, otherwise he will have died in vain."

Just then the Secretary of State's phone rang and as he picked it up, he looked across his expansive desk at his daughter.

"Judith, I thought I gave you instructions not to interrupt me. Oh! I see, then please bring it in."

Turning to Stevie, he said

"Sorry Stevie but there was something I desperately wanted to give you before you left, and it has just arrived."

The door opened and in marched Judith his secretary. It was now two years since Judith had given up her uniform, but she still moved as if she wore one.

"Sir, here is the special delivery that you wanted."

"Thank you, Judith, that will be all." With that she executed a perfect about turn and marched out. At no stage did she look at Stevie or acknowledge her presence.

Stevie stared at the envelope that Judith had just handed her father wondering what it was that his father was going to give her.

"Stevie, I can fully understand that you feel that you owe Chris Smith your life and that you want to repay him in some way. I am just asking, is this the right way to do it? There are very few people who have the capability to be a hostage negotiator. It takes more than the desire to save others."

Stevie looked out of the window at the Washington skyline and thought back to that dark, rancid, foul-smelling room where she was held in Aleppo. She had been captured by the Al-Qaeda group called the Al-Nusra Front while driving a lorry full of aid into the suburbs of Aleppo. She had been determined to prove her father wrong and show that she could care about others. In her mood of defiance, she had not listened to her fellow aid workers who warned her to avoid that area. During the first days of her capture, she was terrified, convinced she was going to be killed or raped or both. The only good news was that her captors saw her as just an ordinary aid worker and never suspected that she was the daughter of the US Secretary of State. They treated her with contempt, barely feeding her, keeping her in a darkened room with no break. Eventually she lost track of time and was becoming more and more dispirited. She found herself swinging between anger at the entire world for allowing her to be treated this way and castigating herself for her stupidity and ignorant pride in not listening to others. Stevie remembered that, after the murder of a fellow captive she was at a particularly low ebb when the door to the cell flew open and Chris was thrown into the room. At the time she had thought that Chris was just another poor bugger like her, and she had not realised that Chris had come to rescue her. Her thoughts returned to the present and her father's question.

"Dad, I have spent the last three months thinking about this. If it wasn't for Chris, I would have been killed by having my throat cut while they made a video for the world to watch. I feel that I have been born again, given a second chance to make something of my life. Before my capture, I only ever thought about myself. It never occurred to me to do something for others without expecting anything in return. Even driving the aid lorry was for me to show you how wrong you were and not to help those who needed the aid. Meeting Chris helped me to see that

5

wanting to help others is important to me and should be my purpose in life."

George McMaster looked at his daughter and saw the change. "Stevie, I do understand, and I do not want to stand in your way. I am just not sure that becoming a hostage negotiator is the best way of doing it."

"Dad, one of the things that I learnt from Chris is that sometimes you have to go with your instincts and mine tell me this is totally the right thing to do."

It was now George McMaster's turn to stare out of the window.

"Stevie, I must admit that I am more than a little anxious about your decision. I have just got you back and I don't want to lose you again. The chances are that you could end up like Chris,"

"Dad, I know but I can't spend my life avoiding my destiny."

George sighed

"And I accept that." He reached over and opened the top drawer of his desk and pulled out a folded piece of paper. Passing it to Stevie, he said

"Here is the telephone number of someone who can put you in touch with the organisation that Chris was part of."

"Thanks Dad."

"And here is the something I wanted to give you. It was sent by Chris's mother and had meant a lot to him."

Stevie opened the envelope and emptied its contents onto her father's desk. Out slid a silver brooch with a decoration etched onto the face of it. Stevie was able to make out a stylised design of a tree covered in a mass of leaves of different shapes and sizes, some of which were falling to earth where they lay rotting and feeding the roots of the tree.

6

"Wow!" Stevie exclaimed "that's fantastic. I can't believe it. I didn't really believe it existed. That is a definite sign that I have made the right decision."

"You know what it is then?"

"Oh yes Dad I know what it is."

Washington – 6 months earlier

George McMaster strode down the corridor towards his office. He had just been in a meeting with the President. George, being a logical man who liked to deal with facts, found the President difficult to communicate with. The President seemed to have the unusual ability to hold two or more opposing opinions in his head at the same time and to feel no need to reconcile them. Depending on the moment, the opinion that came out of the President's mouth seemed to George to be completely random and not based on any kind of analysis. As always, George had left his meeting with the President not knowing what had been decided; luckily the private aides who wrote the minutes usually found a way to make sense of the President's pronouncements.

As George approached his office James Cordwell from the CIA was waiting for him.

"Secretary of State sir, we have found Stevie, but it doesn't look good."

"What do you mean?" George replied sharply.

"I think it is best if you watch this, Sir. I warn you it is not pleasant!" With that James Cordwell stood aside so that the Secretary of State could enter his office and followed with his iPad. When the Secretary of State was seated James Cordwell placed the iPad on the desk in front him and pressed play.

The video started with a close-up of someone young and blond-haired bound in a chair with their head slumped forward. Behind them stood a masked man with a headscarf around his head with Arabic writing visible on it. Next to the masked man stood another young blond-haired captive, also bound, and with their head slumped forward. On the other side of them was another masked man with the same inscribed headscarf. This man had a pistol pointed at the head of the standing captive. Behind them all was a large flag draped across the rear wall. The first masked man started speaking in Arabic becoming more and more agitated. He then grabbed the hair of the seated captive and pulled their head back. George sighed. It was not Stevie, it was a young lad, but his relief lasted no more than a fraction of a second because the masked man suddenly produced a knife and cut the throat of the seated young man. Then, he continued sawing away until he lifted a severed head and shouted his praises to Allah. George McMaster nearly vomited across his massive mahogany desk. The second masked man in the video said something to the other captive, who then lifted their head. This time it was Stevie and George McMaster gasped at the sight of his daughter. To say Stevie looked terrified was an understatement. The masked man, still ranting, pointed at Stevie and then shook the severed head at the camera. The video stopped at this point. George composed himself.

"Do we know what he was shouting about, do we know who they are and where they are?"

James moved around from behind the Secretary of State and sat down in the chair opposite.

"We are still analysing the video but from the translation of what he was saying we believe the masked men are part of a new group called the Al Nusra Front. We have never heard of them before, but they appear to be affiliated to Al Qaeda. They are demanding the return of one of their leaders otherwise they will do to Stevie the same as they did to their other captive."

George McMaster tried to wipe the image of the severed head from mind.

"Do we know who that poor lad they murdered is?"

"Not for sure, but we think it is a young Swedish lad, another aid worker who went missing a month ago."

Shaking his head George tried to think clearly.

"Do we know where their leader is at the moment?"

"He is being held by the Kurds in Northern Syria."

"Do they know who Stevie is?"

"We don't think so otherwise they would be addressing us directly rather than the Western Alliance in general and would be demanding a lot more for her return. Let's hope your daughter has enough sense not to mention it."

"Do you think they know they have a girl and are they likely to rape her?"

"The truth is I don't know the answer to either, I'm afraid."

"She has always been a tomboy so I hope she will go unnoticed. Have they given a deadline?"

"No not really, at the moment I think they are just fishing, trying to get some kind of response."

"OK, what are our options?"

James Cordwell paused momentarily before answering.

"Sir, before we discuss our options, there is another complication?"

"What is it?"

"We have contacted the Kurds through a third-party and they have threatened to kill their captive rather than let him go."

"So, what are our options?" George repeated,

"Given that we don't know where they are holding Stevie, we can't mount a special force rescue mission. If we approach the Al-Nusra Front directly they will realise Stevie is more than just an unlucky aid worker. Also, if we don't first obtain their leader from the Kurds, we haven't got anything to trade with. If we approach the Kurds directly, they are bound to make unreasonable demands of us in exchange for the Al-Nusra leader and may even continue to refuse to let him go."

"So, is there anyone we trust to do it on our behalf?"

"Well, there is an independent private organisation that specialises in these tricky rescue situations. We have used them a couple of times recently."

"Who are they?"

"They don't have a name, just a telephone number."

"Well call them. I want Stevie back alive and well."

"Yes sir" replied the CIA man.

Aleppo 10th October 2016

The room was kept dark but in the late morning some daylight managed to penetrate the cracks between the wood that boarded up the windows. It was enough for Chris and Stevie to be able to see each other. It was during this time each day that Chris talked to Stevie to help keep her spirits up. When Chris had first been thrown in the room Stevie was sat huddled against a wall hugging her knees and did not look up to see who had joined her. This concerned Chris, as it could have been a sign that Stevie had retreated deep inside herself. Chris needed Stevie to be alert and ready to move. Also, he needed to find out what kind of person he was dealing with. His briefing had told him that Stevie was a self-centred, wilful teenager who blamed everyone else but herself for everything wrong in her life. It was Chris that spoke first in a quiet but confident way.

"Stevie, how are you doing? How are you coping with all this?"

Stevie lifted her head. "How do you know my name?"

This was a good sign. At least she was not as locked up inside her head as Chris had feared.

Chris looked Stevie straight in the eyes and replied.

"Because, I have been sent by your father to get you out of here."

Stevie laughed. Another good sign.

"And exactly how are you going to do that? You are a captive just like me."

"We have something that they want, and we want you. We are going to make a trade."

Stevie looked straight back into Chris's eyes assessing the man before her.

"What are you? Some special-forces superhero?"

Chris knew his reply was important to establishing his relationship with Stevie.

"No, I am a volunteer negotiator who specialises in tricky and dangerous situations."

"Do you work for the US Government?"

"No, I am part of a private charitable organisation."

"So how do you know my father?"

"I don't know him personally, but a mutual friend contacted me on his behalf."

"I bet he was pissed off with me?"

"I got the impression he was too concerned and worried to be pissed off."

Chris was pleased that Stevie was asking questions. It showed that she was still thinking and trying to make sense of things."

"Do you have a name?"

"Yes, Chris Smith,"

Just then, there was a sound from outside the door and the sound of men talking loudly in Arabic. Chris moved closer to Stevie.

"Whatever you do, don't let them find out who your father is. It will stop the trade dead in the water and get me killed."

The door flew open and two men carrying assault rifles stepped into the room. They pointed their guns at Stevie and Chris and barked an order in Arabic.

Chris spoke quietly to Stevie.

"I am going with these men. I could be a while. Don't worry though, I will be OK, and I will be back."

The nearest of the two men seemed irritated with Chris for speaking and shook his rifle at him. Chris stepped towards the door in response. The door slammed shut and Stevie was left wondering whether she would see Chris again and if she did, whether his head would still be attached to his body. The sound of the Swedish lad's throat being cut, and the sight of his severed head were always there when she shut her eyes. She never wanted to see that happen again.

As it was, she did see Chris alive and well and it was no more than an hour later when the door was opened, and Chris walked into the room alone rather than being thrown in. The door shut leaving it too dark for Stevie to see Chris.

"So, what was that all about?" muttered Stevie somewhat tersely.

Chris moved closer to where Stevie's voice had come from.

"When I first handed myself over to them, they were suspicious of my motives and didn't trust me. However, I had expected as much so I had brought a letter with me that provided a phone number for them to ring and verify my story."

"Which was?"

"That I was here to negotiate your freedom in return for the freedom of their leader as they had demanded in their video."

"So, who did they ring and how did that verify your story?"

"They rang their leader, and he confirmed it."

"How could they do that?"

"The telephone number that I had given them was for a military base in Northern Iraq where he is being held ready for the exchange."

"So, what happens next?"

"We wait."

Aleppo 11th October 2016

The next morning, they had remained silent until the light came through the cracks again. Stevie looked across at Chris and spoke.

"Are you really who you say you are?" Chris nodded.

It was clear that Stevie was still unsure about letting herself believe that she was being rescued. Chris waited.

"Chris, do you do this all the time?"

"Yes."

Stevie pulled herself up and leant with her back against the wall.

"OK, tell me what was the last situation that you were called upon to negotiate?"

"Ah! That was last week and the first part of your rescue."

"What do you mean, the first part of my rescue?"

"Well, as you know these guys want their leader back. That was why they sent out the video threatening to behead you unless he was freed. The challenge was that he was being held by the Kurds who did not want to free him, in fact they had threatened to kill him rather than let him go. So, I went to negotiate for his release into my care."

"And did you succeed?"

"Yes."

"How did you manage it?"

"Actually, I was very lucky, I discovered something that the Kurd commander wanted more than his prisoner."

"Which was?"

"His little sister, the only remaining member of his family."

"Go on."

"When I first started negotiating with the Kurd leader, I noticed a photo of the girl on his desk and asked him who she was. At first, he didn't want to talk about her, but I persisted which made him angry at first and then suddenly he became very subdued and told me how he and his sister had been separated during a bombing raid and he had searched but never found her. He had never given up hope that she had survived the bombing and was living somewhere in another part of Syria."

"So how did you hope to find her?"

"Well, that was the lucky part. Earlier in the year the Syrian army were holding a small group of Kurdish children as captives and had offered to trade them in return for the Western Allies giving them twenty-four hours to move some of their soldiers out of a small town surrounded by Western forces. I was one of the people who went and collected the children and took them to a holding camp in Iraq. The little girl, Meryem, sat next to me during the journey. I recognised her straight away when I saw her photograph."

Stevie sat there thinking for a while.

"It must have been tricky using her as a bargaining chip?"

"Actually, my instinct told me not to do that, so I took a risk and just had her flown into the Kurdish camp and reunited them without asking for anything in return."

"Wow that was bold! What happened then?"

"The leader was so overwhelmed with gratitude that he gave me his prisoner as a gift."

"I bet the captive was grateful to get away from his captors and to be on the way to being reunited with his men."

"You would think so but in fact he was furious that he, a warrior on a holy mission, was being traded for a small child, even worse, a girl. His pride was severely dented, and he directed his fury at me as the person he held responsible for his humiliation."

Aleppo 12th October 2016

As was becoming the pattern Chris and Stevie waited for the faint light before talking.

"So how did you become a negotiator?"

"Well Stevie, that's an interesting question. Believe it or not, it all started with a book. You know you often hear people say that a book has changed their life but in my case it really did. Much later I discovered that was the intention."

"What do you mean?"

"At the time the book came into my possession I was feeling really unsettled and not at all sure what to do with my life. I needed a change but was struggling to decide what that change should be. There are some people who seem to have clear view of what their future should be but not me. I have never had any sense of purpose or any vision of what my future might hold. I seemed to bounce around like a ball in a pinball machine being directed by unseen flippers and bumpers and not by my own momentum."

"Yes, but what did you mean about the book being intended to change your life?"

"Ah, it seems that I had been identified as a potential recruit by the organisation that I now work for."

"That seems a bit sinister. What happened?"

"It had started when someone witnessed me rescuing a cyclist involved in an accident. They somehow tracked me down and invited me to attend an interview for a job with an emergency rescue charity. What I did not know at the time was that the interview was in fact part of a screening process, to see if I was a potential recruit for the organisation that I now work for. Being given the book was the next step in that process."

I had been for the interview and was on a train returning from London when I was given the book. I was sitting in a very crowded carriage, lost in thought thinking back over the interview.

"So, Chris, what would you say were your major strengths?" the HR Manager had asked, and I had replied,

"Errmm, I am not sure, no I am not at all sure. I seem only ever to see my weaknesses."

"OK" she said sympathetically "and what would you say they were then, Chris?"

"Well, lack of direction, uncertainty in decision making, lack of get up and go."

The HR Manager smiled and looked up at me, I think to see if I was joking. When she realised that I was not, she scribbled something down on her notepad and said "Chris, it is clear, that honesty is one of your strengths."

There was a pause while she glanced back at her notes, then she said,

"What makes you think that working for us is the right thing for you?"

I had shrugged my shoulders.

"The honest answer is I don't know but I want to try it if I can. I have found that I feel so much better when I am helping other people. When I focus on myself, life becomes cloudy and difficult but when I focus on others, especially those in a tricky spot, it all becomes clearer and more straightforward. Also, I find that my energy increases and so do my feelings of self-worth".

It is funny, Stevie, but I could sense a subtle change in the HR Manager at that point. It was as if she had been waiting for this moment. Before she had just been going through the motions. Now, for first time she was paying attention to what I had to say.

"That is interesting, Chris" she said.

"I'd like you to tell me more about that. Can you give me some specific examples of when this has happened?"

"I'll try. I think that the first time that I can remember this happening was when my mother broke both her ankles in a car accident. My father was away on a contract in Dubai and could not get home to take care of me and my little sister or my mother. I think that I was about 9 or 10 years old, and I just knew I had to rise to the situation and look after my mother and my sister, and to stop my father from worrying. That was the first time that I found a real sense of purpose in life. I had an unlimited supply of energy. This went on for about 6 weeks, doing the shopping, cooking, caring, cleaning, and washing. I did that as well as going to school and making sure that my sister was coping. When my mother was able take over again, I remember feeling very proud of myself, but I also remember feeling a sense of loss now that my help was not needed anymore."

The HR Manager brushed a hair from her face and leant forward.

17

"I see, and have you experienced anything similar recently".

I had to stop and think.

"Yes, funnily enough something like this happened just last week. I was in Bristol, and I was walking down Gloucester Road when I saw a cyclist come off his bike and fall under a car. It was an awful thing to see. The car driver managed to stop but the cyclist seemed wedged under the car. This happened in front of a crowd of people at a bus stop and the road was extremely busy with traffic, but nobody did anything. The driver was on her mobile trying to contact the emergency services and everyone else was just watching. I knew instantly that I had to do something, so I got down on the ground and crawled under the car and spoke the cyclist. He was conscious and managed to tell me that he was in no pain but was having difficulty breathing as the backpack he was wearing was pressing down on him under the weight of the car. He was becoming distressed, he felt as if he was being suffocated. I checked around him and could see that, apart from his backpack pinning him to the floor, there was no contact between him and the car. I crawled out from under the car and reassured the driver that the cyclist was still alive and could be rescued. I then walked over to the bus queue and selected four or five men and lads who looked reasonably fit and urged them to help me by lifting the car up off the cyclist while I crawled under again to see if I could free him. When I reached him, he was losing consciousness, so I kept talking to him while the car was lifted a few inches. This was enough to relieve the pressure on him, so he could breathe properly again. I then crawled backwards, dragging him with me. It was a real struggle to move him but as he began to move, he realised what was happening and began to crawl as well. We emerged from under the car as a fire engine and ambulance arrived and basically took over. There was a lot of clapping from the bus queue and other passers-by and many of them came over and shook my hand and slapped me on the back. The police took a statement from me and I left feeling that I had done something really worthwhile."

The HR Manager sat back in her chair.

"Chris, I think that was an impressive thing that you did, and you should be proud of yourself. What you did took a great deal of courage. So, are you saying that apart from these moments when you are helping others, your normal day to day life does not make you feel that you are doing anything worthwhile? Is that correct?"

"Yes, it is as if I need somebody to have an emergency that I can respond to before I come alive. Most days are a waste of time really. Most of the time, I feel lost with no sense of direction."

As I said this, the HR Manager nodded in acknowledgement and turning a page of her notes said,

"Is that why your work history in your application seems so disjointed?"

"Probably"

"Perhaps we could talk about your work history now?"

"Sure"

"Can we start with your decision to leave university during your first year to go and work on a building site? Why did you do that?"

I shook my head as I knew this question would come up. I also knew I did not have a satisfactory answer.

"I think it was caused by the fact that I suddenly realised that I had only gone to university to fulfil my parent's ambitions. My Mum and Dad are great and have always loved me and wanted the best for me and I have always wanted to please them in return. So, I ended up studying Economics at university when I had not the slightest interest in Economics."

Frowning, she said "But why start working on a building site?"

I laughed "You know how it is? I had a mate who, at the time, was saving up to go travelling and told me that it was a good place to work to earn money."

19

"And was it?"

"Yes, and I enjoyed the work but as it turned out I was not particularly bothered about earning money and the builders that I was working with all seemed to dislike me for having gone to university. They made my life very unpleasant with snide comments, practical jokes, stuff like that. So, I left and went into a call centre."

"What made you choose a call centre?" she said not quite able to keep the incredulity out of her voice.

"I didn't really. A friend of my father was a manager there and my father asked him if he could find me a job. My mother and father were determined that I should have a career with prospects and not be a manual labourer. As always, they wanted the best for me."

"So how did you find working at the call centre?"

"I hated it!"

"Why was that?"

"Greed! Everyone, including my team leader and in fact the whole call centre was driven by what it needed to achieve, their objectives, their rewards, regardless of what the people that they were calling wanted. I was uncomfortable with the targets and pep talks and clapping when someone was able to talk their prospect into buying something they did not want. When I got on the phone, I found it impossible to stick to the script that I was supposed to follow. I wanted to find out about the individual I was talking to and whether the things I was selling were likely to be of use to them."

"So, you eventually left?"

"The truth is that I was fired. Apparently, I didn't have the competencies required for the job and in addition they said I had an attitude problem. Probably because I kept refusing to apply pressure on the people, that I was calling, to make a decision to buy while I was still on the phone."

At this point I remembered the HR Manager closing her note pad, gathering up her pens and saying

"Thanks, Chris, from what I can see the rest of your work history seems to follow the same pattern. So, I must ask you, why should it be any different if you come to work for us?"

I remember just shrugging and replying "I am sorry, but I don't have an answer. I suspect that I will only know the answer to that question once I have tried it."

With that she stood up and held out her hand.

"Well Chris, thank you for sparing the time to come and see me. Also thank you for answering my questions so honestly. I need to have some conversations internally and I will get back to you within a week", and that was that. The interview had only lasted thirty minutes.

Stevie, as I thought back over the interview, I realised that I had not asked any questions about what the job entailed. Here I was applying for a job with the emergency rescue charity having been contacted by a stranger. You would have thought that I would be extremely curious and want to find out as much as I could about the role and the organisation. But I had just concentrated on answering her questions as best I could and nothing else. This lack of purpose or direction was typical of me at this point in my life, and I was left with no idea of how I had done. I would just have to await her call.

Anyway, the point is, I was so engrossed in thinking about the interview that I had not really noticed the person next to me on the train, except that he was reading a very old looking book. Nothing else about him had registered. When the train arrived at Reading, he asked me to let him out as this is was his stop, so I stood up and moved out of his way, not really taking any notice of him. Just as he moved away, he turned and handed me his book and simply said

"You should read this!" before turning away to get off the train. I retook my seat and studied the book. The first thing that I noticed was how heavy it was. It was bound in old dark brown leather with lots of embossing on the cover. It was quite thick and well worn. It struck me as being valuable and that puzzled me. Why would someone give a stranger something that was valuable? I sat staring at the book for a while. Part of me wanted to look inside it there and then. Another part of me seemed to be enjoying resisting that urge. I had a premonition that this book was important and could have a big influence on my life. I decided to keep it closed until I got home.

Later that evening I sat down in my chair and started to study the book further. I'll admit Stevie, I was extremely curious and a little bit excited. Firstly, I smelt the leather binding. It had a bitter-sweet odour of old leather chairs and musty bookshops. Looking closely at it in a bright light I could see there was an embossed design of some sort covering it. By holding the book at an angle to the light I could make out a stylised shape of a tree. The embossing on the cover was in delicate detail and hard to see given how well-worn the book was. Finally, I opened the book. The first page just had a title printed on it. No author or publisher or any other details. I looked at the title "The Seeker of Purpose". This immediately struck a chord with me given where I was at that stage of my life."

Stevie stood up and walked around. The light was going, and she was lost in thinking through what Chris had just been telling her.

"Chris, do think the book being given to you and your interview were connected?"

Out of the gloom Chris replied. "Yes, definitely."

"What makes you so certain?"

22

"I found out later that it was a deliberate and planned step in a recruitment process. It had two functions. The first was to engage my attention with the idea of dedicating my life to helping others and the second was to test my motives if I chose to move to the next step."

"What was the book about?"

"A medieval boy called Aelfgar and his father, Aethelwulf. It starts with Aelfgar running away from his violent and dominating uncle to try to find his missing father. Along the way he meets people who help him to overcome various obstacles on his quest, including being pursued by his uncle's henchman. He eventually finds his father and discovers that he had suffered a nervous breakdown and had been rebuilding his life. The boy reflects upon his life before and after running away and on his father's past and in doing so he uncovers some lessons to be learnt from both sets of experiences. As a result, he identifies that his purpose in life is to help the needy in every way he can and to find ways to counteract evil when he can."

Chris stopped speaking for a while and they both sat in the dark lost in their own thoughts. At this point their food was shoved through the door and even though it was usually revolting to eat they both scrambled across the floor in the dark to find it. After a while, some plastic bottles of water were put through the door and their metal dishes were removed. As they both drank their bottles of water Stevie thought about the book and its role in Chris becoming a negotiator and his ending up in this cell with her.

"Earlier you said that the book changed your life. How did it do that?"

Chris was encouraged that Stevie seemed genuinely interested and absorbed in his tale, so he made the decision to tell her more.

"Well, having read the book I called a telephone number as instructed at the end of the book. I was invited by the person on the other end to meet them and return the book. A few days later I went to an address that I had been given on the telephone. The building was a large Victorian house in the middle of Kensington and looked deserted. I initially thought that there had been a mistake but as I approached, the door opened, and I was invited to enter the house by a large man dressed in black. Inside, the room I was taken to was unfurnished except for a large wooden table and seated at the table was a smartly dressed woman. The man led me to the table and indicated that I should sit at the chair opposite her. After I had done so, he returned to stand by the door through which I had entered. The woman waited until I was seated and then welcomed me and asked if I had read the book. When I said that I had read every word, she started to ask me questions regarding its contents. Then she asked about the thoughts and feelings I had when reading it. By the time that I had answered all her questions I felt drained and weary, but she was not finished with me. She explained that I had made a positive impression upon her and that she would like to arrange a further meeting so she could introduce me to some of her colleagues. Unlike my HR interview, this time I had hundreds of questions I wanted to ask her and I was determined to get some answers. We spent the next hour with me asking my questions and her answering them. When I had arrived at the meeting, I had been curious and intrigued about why I had been given the book and what might happen from my having read it. By the time I had had all my questions answered I was well and truly hooked and so started my journey of self-discovery, self-sacrifice, and personal fulfilment within the Tree of Life organisation. From that day onwards all confusion and self-doubt disappeared, to be replaced with certainty, commitment, and a true sense of purpose. I now live to save the lives of others by rescuing them from dangerous situations. It is what I was born to do".

As Stevie listened to Chris telling his story, she had a myriad of questions she wanted to ask Chris but they both were tired so they spoke no more that day, not knowing that tomorrow Chris would be dead.

Chapter 2

Small Moments

Jerusalem 638CE

Aileran finished drying the feet of the last of this group of pilgrims. They had travelled from Medina in Hejaz to pray at the place where Muhammad ascended to heaven. As Aileran stood up he asked the group if they had somewhere to stay the night. They replied that they did not, so he directed them to the nearby mosque where he knew that the local Iman would provide them with food and shelter. Aileran reflected on the fact that whatever the faith of the pilgrims that he met and welcomed to Jerusalem, they were always grateful for his help and attention. He had been going to the main gates of the city early every morning, waiting for them to be opened to allow in the first visitors of the day. There he would stay until the gates closed at the end of the day. He had been doing this for a year and still felt fulfilled in his self-appointed role. He hoped that there would be someone like him awaiting his entry into heaven to soothe his weary soul and help him to acclimatise to his new surroundings. Someone to help with the transition from "travelling towards" to "arriving at".

Looking up he saw a new group of pilgrims approaching the city gates. By the way they were dressed, he guessed that they were from Northern Europe. He stepped forward to meet them with a bowed head and a welcoming smile.

"Welcome" he said, "You must be thirsty after your travels. Would you like some water?"

There were six people in the group, four men and two women. Each carried a carved wooden cross suspended by a leather thong around their neck and small packs on their backs. Each also leaned on a sturdy wooden staff. One of the men was clearly having difficulty walking and was being supported by one of his companions. They stopped before him and exchanged glances before one of them spoke.

"Thank you, some water would be most welcome."

Aileran reached behind him into the doorway and produced some wooden cups which he distributed to the group and then he filled each cup from a pitcher of water. He could not help but notice that the man who had been supported by his friends was shaking and having difficulty standing. Aileran took the wooden stool that he used when washing the feet of arriving pilgrims and placed it in front of the man.

"Perhaps your companion would like to rest a while before entering the city." The group helped the man down on to the stool and then they all sipped their cups of water in silence. Aileran stood back as he always did and observed the group. The man now sitting on the stool looked unwell. The rest of his companions looked weary but healthy.

Aileran waited until they had finished drinking their water then, without asking, he knelt before the man sitting on the stool and began removing the man's sandals. Taking the pitcher of water, he poured some over the man's feet and taking some cloth from the folds of his habit he began washing them. The effect on the man was remarkable. The frown of discomfort on his face was replaced with a smile of serenity. One by one Aileran washed the feet of each member of the group to equal effect. When he was done Aileran suggested that they take the sick man to the Tree of Life hospital where he would be looked after. He gave them directions and sent them on their way.

There were no more pilgrims that morning and this allowed Aileran time to sit on his stool at the city gates and reminisce about the past. Who would have thought that the decision to commit to becoming a "Peregrini pro amore Dei." would lead to him washing the feet of strangers here in Jerusalem? Looking back on his life so far, Aileran found it hard to decide whether it was made up of a series of fortuitous accidents or whether it was a prescribed design set by God. Either way, he felt grateful he had reached a point in life where he felt completely at one with God.

He had started life in poverty and had got used to working hard from an early age. His parents were farmers, and he was their sixth child. Two of his elder siblings had died and were subsequently replaced by two younger ones. Life was extremely hard for his parents and when he was seven years old, they were forced to send him to Clonard Monastery to become a monk as they could not look after everyone. The older boys could work on the farm, the older girls could be married off. The younger ones still needed to be cared for, but he was old enough to fend for himself. In the monastery as a child, he recognised that his circumstances had improved and he tried to make the most of his opportunity. He saw the necessity of leaving home and at least in the monastery he would be fed. He studied hard and took notice of advice given to him by the elder monks. Now, looking back, he saw how fortunate he had been. In the monastery he had been educated and had learnt about the world outside Clonard, none of which would have happened if he had stayed on the farm. Initially, he found it hard, if not impossible to make any connection with a God who seemed to be this remote, autocratic figure giving out rules and requiring people to earn his love. Later, when he was studying the early life of Jesus, he began to see God differently. He saw that God was waiting with open arms for individuals to find their way to reach him. He also realised that many of the rules that he instinctively rebelled against were set by men and not God. He stayed in the Monastery in Clonard until he was sixteen and then he was sent to Cantwaraburh to study. He was part of a mission sent to understand how the Roman church differed from the Celtic church.

While at Cantwaraburh Abbey he discovered a copy of "The Consolation of Philosophy" by Boethius. Reading this gave him a new perspective and caused him to look at himself differently and to start to question himself, his life and why he could not find his way to God. After returning to Clonard Monastery, he began to peel back everything that he had been taught and discover a way to move forward. Then one day, it became crystal clear to him that the monks around him spent too much time intellectualising about what God wants us to be and not enough time allowing God to show us and he realised that if he stayed in the enclosed world of the monastery his chances of finding a way to God were limited. After many deep discussions with the Abbot of the monastery, he decided that he needed to just put himself wholly into the hands of God and adopt a life of Peregrinatio pro Christo. Aileran, with his background and character, had always been drawn to the early teachings of Jesus and those of John the Baptist and their ascetic lifestyle and message. He felt that hiding away in comfort from the world contemplating the gospels was wasting his life and bringing no benefit to the world. He decided that leaving Ireland, not just the Monastery was the best way to open himself to God's will. He had many more discussions with the Father Abbot who suggested that rather than wander aimlessly as some Peregrini did, Aileran should select an initial destination and allow time during the journey for God to show himself. Aileran found a quiet spot in the cloisters to think and almost immediately and with no fuss, the word Jerusalem appeared in his mind. Not long after that he left the Monastery in Clonard and began his journey toward Jerusalem. When in towns and villages he begged for alms and in the countryside, he lived off the land finding berries, fungi, and small creatures. At first, he experienced waves of exhilaration followed by periods of doubt and fear. Gradually his mood settled, and he stopped thinking about himself and began observing the world around him. Now, as he sat here in Jerusalem all these years later, contemplating his journey from Clonard, he recalled the various small moments along the way that had a big impact on his way of looking at the world and eventually finding God.

Rheims

Aileran approached Rheims feeling tired and hungry. He had not eaten for two days and was struggling to keep going. Ahead of him, he could see a group of people and could hear bugles and drums being played loudly. As he got closer to the crowd it became clear that in the centre there was a large party of clerics who were gathered around someone sat on a throne. When he was still a little way off, one of the clerics broke away from the group and hurried towards Aileran.

"Welcome to Rheims, brother, you look as if you have travelled far. Are you on a pilgrimage?" Aileran nodded and leant heavily on his staff. The cleric came alongside Aileran and placed his arm around Aileran and took some of his weight.

"Please come with me brother, as Bishop Auric would like to welcome you to Rheims and bless you on your journey." The cleric led Aileran towards the crowd. They joined a small queue of fellow pilgrims. Aileran was feeling very light-headed and somewhat detached from the scene around him. Moving closer, he could see that the seated man was obviously Bishop Auric because was dressed in his full regalia including an ornate shepherd's crook. As each pilgrim approached, one of the clerics would speak quietly to the pilgrim and then shout out their name, where they had travelled from and destination. The pilgrim would then kneel before the seated Bishop Auric, receive his blessing and be led to one side, where they were given a cup of water and a piece of bread. Each traveller was then led to a stool where one of the clerics would wash the pilgrim's feet. Soon it was Aileran's turn and before he knew it, he was seated on the stool having his feet washed as he ate his bread and drank his water. Immediately he began to revive and felt grateful to Bishop Auric and his group of clerics for their welcome and generosity. It turned out that there were no more pilgrims arriving after Aileran and for a while he sat and watched the activity around him. Bishop Auric stood and some of the clerics picked up his throne and placed it on a nearby cart. The bugles and drums started up again and Bishop Auric and his entourage marched off in the direction of the Cathedral. Within minutes Aileran and the other pilgrims were alone and slightly bemused to have been scooped up into what seemed be a passing church ceremony. Aileran sat there, unsure of his feelings about the event. Initially he had felt grateful to have been given food and drink at a time when he desperately needed both. Also, the experience of having his feet washed had revived his spirit in the same way the food and drink had revived his body. However, he had the uneasy feeling that the acts of seeming generosity were contrived to provide an opportunity for Bishop Auric to feel good about himself and convince the crowd of his virtuous nature. Aileran felt guilty for having these feelings when he had just benefited from the whole event and it had not really cost him anything but his time. Eventually, Aileran set off again, heading into the city and before long he caught up with one of the other pilgrims. As Aileran drew alongside the man they nodded to each other in acknowledgement. The man was much older than Aileran and had lost an eye at some stage in his life. He spoke a crude kind of Latin but enough that Aileran could understand him.

"What did you make of all that?" he asked. Aileran thought for a moment.

"To be honest, I am not sure. While I was grateful for the food and water, I was left feeling that it was not given genuinely."

"Ha! Well said, Brother! You have just summed up my feelings too! It felt as if we were only being given it to show how generous and caring Bishop Auric was and not because we were in need. It seemed that too much attention was being drawn to an act of charity that would be better served if done privately. I have been on pilgrimage for most of my life and I have seen many acts of genuine charity. In Antwerp I have seen the wives of wealthy merchant's exchange clothing with their maids to become anonymous, then go to the local pauper's hospital to care for the unfortunate and then return home but never tell anyone where they have been. That to me is genuine goodness and highlights the falseness of today's act of self-aggrandisement."

Aileran thought about those words and that day's events many times over during his journey and every time ended up with the same thought. It had been wonderful to be provided with food and drink on arrival at a new town or city and this feeling was multiplied by the act of having his feet washed. What a shame that it was soiled by the fact it was not a genuine charitable act. Recalling that event now made Aileran even more determined to continue his service to arriving pilgrims focused on their needs and not his own, and it served to remind him to be forever humble.

Pavia

Shortly after arriving in Pavia, he stepped into the tiny church of St Columban and immediately felt at home. It was sparsely decorated with a minimal design. The altar at the far end was simple and plain and in front of it, knelt in prayer, was a single nun. Her habit matched the church in its simplicity and plainness. Aileran stood silently just inside the doorway, not wishing to disturb the nun's concentration. After a few minutes, the nun crossed herself and stood up. She turned and still locked in her thoughts, looked up and saw Aileran. She gave a start and crossed herself again. Aileran spoke quietly.

"I am sorry to startle you, Sister. I did not want to interrupt your prayer."

The nun looked at this imposing monk who was at least twice her height and had the most impressive head and beard of flaming red hair.

"Please Brother, there is no need for you to apologise. I was just praying to St Columban and for a moment I thought you were him coming to bless me. We don't get many visitors here so that added to the surprise."

Aileran smiled.

"Sister, I must apologise again, this time for not being your Saint coming to visit you." Now it was the nun who smiled.

"Do I detect from your accent that you are Irish like our Saint, maybe he sent you after all? Why have you come to this tiny church when not many people do?" With that she sat down on one of the benches and gestured for Aileran to do the same. Once he had settled himself, he answered her question.

"Well Sister, the short of it is that I have heard that Severus Boethius is buried here and I want to visit his grave and pay my respects." As soon as Aileran mentioned Boethius's name the nun's face lit up with pleasure.

"My name is Sister Antonia and I am a direct descendant of Severus Boethius. One of my duties is to tend my ancestor's grave. May I ask your name and why you have gone out of your way to pay your respects to him?"

"Sister Antonia, my name is Aileran and I have left Ireland and placed my life in the hands of God. I am travelling to Jerusalem and my route passes through here in Pavia and I had heard along the way that Severus Boethius was interred here. As to why I wanted to pay my respects, that is because my reading "The Consolation of Philosophy" by your ancestor was a major influence in my decision to leave the monastery in Clonard and travel across the world. His wisdom and clear thinking lifted the veil clouding my vision and allowed me to glimpse my destiny." Sister Antonia stood up suddenly.

"I would love to hear how my ancestor's writing achieved that but first let me take you to his grave." She led Aileran beyond the altar and through a low door into a tiny room with just enough space for a bed, table and shrine to the Mother Mary. The room had just one small window high up in the far wall and below it was a door so small that Aileran doubted that he would be able to pass through it. However, when opened, it revealed a recess that contained a stone coffin laid upon a stone shelf. The coffin was plain and undecorated except for a small name plate inscribed with the words Severini Boethius. Sister Antonia made the sign of the cross and stood back to allow Aileran to approach. Aileran was suddenly overcome with emotion and fell to his knees and began to pray silently. Deep inside he felt himself let go of all conscious thought and just be. It was as if he were floating in the air and was being washed from head to toe in a golden light. Gradually he became aware of his surroundings again and rose unsteadily to his feet. He felt exhausted but at the same time ecstatic. Sister Antonia seemed to understand and gently led him back to the bench where they had sat earlier. She poured him a cup of refreshing water and waited until he had composed himself. Aileran looked at Sister Antonia and shook his head slowly

"I am not sure what happened then. I seemed to be lifted out of my body. I am left feeling euphoric. I have never felt like this before." Sister Antonia looked up to the ceiling for a few moments before replying.

"That has happened to me a few times, I am happy to say. I believe that your soul wants you to know that your decision to leave your monastery and travel was the right decision. You are on the right path." They sat in silence for a while and then Sister Antonia continued.

"Before I became a nun, I was a member of the local aristocracy. From my childhood I felt that I was different from everyone around me. They all seemed to be lost in politics, ambition, and achievements whereas all I ever seem to want was privacy and solitude. I found this by attending church and listening to the word of God. Luckily for me I have never been an attractive woman and with my reclusiveness added to that fact it that meant my father never held any thoughts of marrying me off for gain. So, when I suggested that I enter the nunnery he did not stand in my way. After I had been a nun for just over a year, I was sent to prepare this church before it was opened for St Columban's day. As I swept the floor a shaft of bright sunlight shone through the open door. Outside the birds were singing joyfully and I had an experience just as you described. At that moment I knew I had chosen the right path. I had always thought that it would take big moments in my life to experience God, but I eventually found him in little moments like that, or when handing food to the poor, or tending a sick person who needs my help. For you it seems, God is somewhere else, but for me he is here in this tiny church. Aileran studied Sister Antonia's face and could see her inner peace. She excused herself and wishing him safe travels, she retreated to the room containing Boethius's tomb. After her departure Aileran sat quietly for a short while before he left to continue his journey. From that moment on Aileran looked at the world differently. Instead of waiting for some grand divine intervention in his life that would reveal God to him, he now looked for the small things that show God's presence. He watched as buds appeared on the trees and bushes in the Spring, how first thing in the morning the birds would sing as the sun rose on another day. He took pleasure in the kindness of strangers and the simple exchange of "Please" and "Thank You" when begging for his daily meal.

Now he was settled here in Jerusalem he thought about that brief meeting with Sister Antonia and how in front of the resting place of Severus Boethius he had experienced that small moment of ecstasy. The moment had not lasted long but the effect was powerful. Was that God showing himself or simply his soul telling him that he was on his way to successfully finding his place in the world?

Rome

Another small moment happened in Rome. Aileran stood at the back of Church of San Paolo fuori le Mura watching as the congregation listened to the words of the officiating priest. As always during a service, Aileran felt disconnected from the people and the event. The priest was reading the bible and was quoting St Paul. Aileran thought back to his lessons on St Paul back in Clonard. He remembered thinking then that without St

Paul travelling and preaching the story of Jesus, there would have been no St Patrick and that without St Patrick the Christian faith might never have reached Ireland. That would have meant there would have been no monastery to provide him with a home when he needed one. Both St Paul and St Patrick had been Apostles taking Jesus's message to far off peoples. Aileran had never felt confident enough in his search for God to want to preach to others and because of this he had never felt the need or desire to be an evangelist. His travels were all about finding God for himself and not about being an apostle. Back in his lessons in Clonard, the one fact about St Paul that had had the greatest effect on Aileran was that St Paul had been converted to Christianity not by the deeds or words of other men, but by direct contact with Jesus in a vision. This had instinctively appealed to Aileran, and he had originally sought a similar direct relationship for himself. This desire for a direct dramatic moment of enlightenment, as had happened to St Paul, may have prevented his being open to smaller, simpler opportunities that had passed him by. Thanks to Sister Antonia, this was no longer the case. Back in the church, the priest conducting the service began dispensing the Holy Communion. As each member of the congregation received Holy Communion, Aileran studied their faces and witnessed the peace and tranquillity that settled upon them. He could see that the service and the ritual of Holy Communion was helping members of the congregation to access their God. Even after many years in the monastery and numerous church services on his journey, Holy Communion had always failed to do the same to him. He did not move forward to take Holy Communion because he would have felt hypocritical if he did. He felt that he would have been disrespectful to the congregation and the priest; for whilst it was empty of God for him, it clearly was full of God for them. For him now, the world was his church and his travelling through it had become a kind of communion. Since his conversation with Sister Antonia in Pavia, he had seen for the first time that God was there all around him and clear to be seen by anyone who took the trouble to look. After a short while, he continued his journey.

Thessaloniki

Aileran awoke suddenly, not sure what had demanded his attention. He sat up, silence. Then he heard it again, a scream of fear and agony. Leaping to his feet he ran to the mouth of the cave. The cave was high up a rock face overlooking the road from Dyrrhachium to Thessaloniki. There below him was a group of men kicking what appeared to be an old sack. The scream came again and Aileran realised that it was not a sack but a man. Aileran ran to the back of the cave, and picked up his wooden staff, and then clambered down to the road and rushed towards the group of men. They stopped kicking the man and looked up as he approached. Before any of them could react, he swung his staff and brought it down across the back of the nearest man who grunted and dropped to one knee. His nearest companion held a club which he swung viciously at Aileran, who saw it coming and leapt to one side. The gang of attackers had the advantage of numbers, but Aileran had two advantages that soon began to tell. The first was his appearance; for he was a giant of a man and had a wild look about him. The second and in the end the most important, was that having two much older brothers had meant he had learnt to fight competently from a young age. Stepping forward towards the man who had just missed Aileran's head, he thumped his staff down onto his foot. This time the scream came from the attacker and not his victim on the floor. As Aileran raised his staff again he felt an excruciating pain in his elbow and his arm went numb. His staff fell to the ground. Turning, he saw one of the two remaining men raising his club to strike him again. Aileran sidestepped the blow and with his good arm landed a punch on the man's temple, making him stagger and shake his head. The remaining man said something, then tore a bag from the man on the floor and ran off in the direction of Pella, followed by the rest of them. Aileran watched them go and then knelt by the man who lay still on the floor. Aileran could see why he originally thought the men were kicking a sack, for the man was bundled up in sackcloth and was covered in mud. As a passing gesture of revenge, the man with the broken foot had turned back then stooped to the ground,

36

picked up a stone and thrown it as hard as he could towards Aileran. At the same time, the sack man on the floor suddenly cried out in pain, Aileran looked down momentarily and, as he did so, the stone hit him on the back of the head, and everything went black.

Aileran started to regain consciousness. He could feel himself gently rocking from side to side and he could make out the sound of horse's hooves on the road. He opened his eyes and tried to sit up, but a wave of nausea caused him to lay back and close his eyes again. He lay there a while trying to make sense of his situation. He could hear someone talking as if to themselves. He did not recognise the language but the tone was calming and encouraging. He gently turned his head in the direction of the voice and very warily, he opened his eyes. The pain and nausea swept over him again but not so overwhelmingly as before. He could see that he was laying on the back of a horse-drawn cart and that the voice was that of the driver talking to his horse as they went along. Aileran heard a movement to his left and accompanied by another wave of pain and nausea he turned to look in the direction of the sound. Laying there beside him was the man who he had seen being attacked. He was still unconscious but seemed to be breathing regularly. The driver turned around and spoke to Aileran, but Aileran could not recognise even one word that was said. Aileran lay there for a while with his eyes closed, fighting the desire to vomit. The cart driver said something to the horse who turned and left the road. Immediately the cart started bouncing violently and almost in unison Aileran and the man beside him cried out in pain. Shortly the cart came to a halt and the cart driver jumped down and shouted to someone in an urgent manner. He heard the voice of a woman reply, then felt someone tugging at his ankles. He tried to sit up to see what was happening but immediately passed out with a pain that exploded inside his head. Later he awoke and found himself under a pile of furs at the rear of a dark room. Sat on a stool close to the fire was a woman looking directly at him. When she saw that Aileran was awake a large smile appeared on her face and she took a ladle from a shelf and picking up a large mug filled it with a broth of some kind that had been simmering in a pot over the fire. She came over to Aileran and after helping him to sit up she passed the cup to Aileran and still with a huge smile on her face, she gestured for him to drink it. Aileran smiled back, partly out of courtesy but mainly from the anticipation of enjoying some warm food. The woman watched as Aileran took his first sip. Aileran had now learnt to treasure these small moments because they were rare. His earlier smile grew into a large grin and lifting the cup in acknowledgement he uttered "Thank you" in Gaelic. The woman seemed pleased with his response. She then turned and went to see how the unconscious man was. He was lying still and seemed to be comfortable and relaxed. The woman returned and said something to Aileran before picking up a basket and leaving the room. Aileran sat there; having finished his broth he reflected on his situation. It seemed that he and the man in sackcloth had been found by the cart driver and loaded on to his cart and brought here to his house and that he and his wife were looking after them. Looking around the room it was clear that they had little in the way of possessions and lived a frugal lifestyle. Aileran took stock of his injuries, both of which were throbbing painfully. It was clear to him that it would be a while before he would be able to continue his journey. This thought made him feel uncomfortable about his being a burden on the couple. His thinking was interrupted by a cry of pain behind him. He managed to stand up and make his way shakily to the man who seemed to be dreaming and was tossing and turning in his sleep. Aileran found a cloth and dampened it with some water from a bucket. He dabbed the man's forehead gently and this seemed to calm him. He was still sitting there next to the injured man when the man and his wife returned accompanied by a priest of the Orthodox church. The priest was tall, almost as tall as Aileran and was also blue eyed, but unlike Aileran's his hair was pale gold in colour. The priest and the cart driver exchanged glances and the priest spoke to Aileran in Latin.

"Hello brother, my name is Father Gregor, and I am the local priest. Nicolas and Sophia, your hosts, are members of my flock. How is the injured man, is he still unconscious?"

"Yes Father, he is, he seems to be in a deep sleep."

"May I see him as I have some knowledge of healing and may be able to help."

Aileran stood aside and let the priest kneel at the man's side. Father Gregor examined the man thoroughly and reaching into a large bag that he had slung over his shoulder, he produced a small bottle. As he removed a cork from the bottle, he turned to Aileran.

"May I ask your name?"

"Of course, my name is Aileran, and I am from Clonard in Ireland."

"Ah! Are you a Peregrini?"

"Yes Father, I am on my way to Jerusalem."

"What is this poor man's name?"

"I do not know. He has been unconscious since I rescued him from a group of bandits."

"I see. I had made the assumption that you were travelling together."

"No, Father." Aileran explained to Father Gregor how he had been woken by the man's screams, had managed to rescue him and how the cart driver must have come along and brought them both to this cottage.

Father Gregor turned back to the man and held the small bottle under the man's nose. Instantly the man jerked his head away and started coughing and then opened his eyes. He stared at Father Gregor and then Aileran and tried to sit up. Father Gregor gently restrained him while the patient tried to understand what was happening to him. Father Gregor said something, and the woman brought a cup of water to the man, who was still looking around trying to make sense of his situation. Father Gregor took the cup and held it to the man's lips. The man took a sip and as he continued to drink the refreshing water he visibly became more at ease. When he had emptied the cup, he looked around and spoke gently. Aileran did not recognise the words, nor it appeared did the couple whose cottage they were in. However, it seemed that Father Gregor did, for he broke into the broadest grin and replied excitedly. After a lengthy exchange, Father Gregor turned to Aileran and explained that the man's name was Solomon, and he was from Colonia in the land of the Franks. He was of the Jewish faith and, like Aileran, was on pilgrimage to Jerusalem. Father Gregor went on to explain that he too was from Colonia originally. He said that he had told Solomon of how Aileran had rescued him and how the cart driver had brought him here and that Solomon wanted to express his gratitude to everyone for caring about his welfare. Aileran said that he was only too happy to have been able to help. Aileran then asked Father Gregor if he would look at his own injuries. Father Gregor examined Aileran's elbow and was confident that there were no broken bones, but it was badly bruised and swollen. There was a swelling on the back of Aileran's head where the stone had hit it and a nasty gash which was weeping blood. Father Gregor delved into a large shoulder bag that he had brought with him and extracted an assortment of herbs. He then used these to make a paste which he applied to Aileran's and Solomon's wounds. When he had finished, Aileran spoke to Father Gregor about his concern that he was unable repay the kindness being shown to him and Solomon. He said that he was planning to continue his journey as soon as he could but was worried that until then he and Solomon would be a burden upon the cart driver and his wife. As a Peregrini he carried no money or anything of value to pay them. Father Gregor smiled and stood up and walked over to the couple and spoke to them for some time. When the conversation ended, the three of them came over to Aileran and Father Gregor spoke.

"Nicolas and Sophia have asked me to tell you that they appreciate your thinking of them in this time of distress for you. They want me to tell you that it is their responsibility, their duty and desire to help anyone in need that crosses their path. They believe that if they do good and help others in this life then their reward will come in the next life. They want you and Solomon to know that you are welcome to stay with them for as long as you require to regain your health."

"Please tell them that I thank them with all my soul and that I am sorry that I have no means to repay them for their kindness."

Father Gregor stepped forward and spoke to the couple quietly and gently. Father Gregor returned to Aileran and was smiling as he translated their reply.

"Nicholas says if you wish to repay our kindness, then please take the first opportunity on your travels to help someone in need of your assistance."

Aileran smiled and touched the wooden cross around his neck. Father Gregor returned to Solomon's side and began explaining the conversation whilst examining his handiwork in treating Solomon's bruising.

Aileran sat there watching Father Gregor and he could see how much Father Gregor cared about making Solomon well again. He instantly recalled his conversation with Sister Antonia and how she told him that she found God in similar moments. It occurred to Aileran that apart from rescuing Solomon from the gang of thieves he had not really helped anyone since he left Ireland. It was at this point on his journey that the two ideas of giving help to those who needed it and the earlier experience of being welcomed into Rheims by being given food and water and of having his feet washed started to become the germ of an idea that later became his way of glimpsing God.

A week later Aileran said his goodbyes to Nicholas and Sophia. A few days earlier Father Gregor and Nicholas had taken Solomon by cart to Thessaloniki Synagogue to be cared for by the Jewish community. As Aileran strode away from the cottage where he had been cared for and shown such kindness, his mind went back to the Bishop of Pavia and his ostentatious display of charity. True charity is given quietly, he thought, as he compared the actions of the bishop to those of Nicholas and Sophia. He also reflected on Father Gregor and his genuine concern for the wellbeing of Aileran and Solomon. It occurred to Aileran that it was important to see people clearly through their actions and not to be misled by their position in life.

Constantinople

When Aileran arrived in Constantinople, he witnessed a heated argument between two groups of clergymen as he was passing through a large square on his way to catch the ferry across to Anatolia. The square was full of various groups of clergymen in a variety of attire; it appeared that something was about to take place, so Aileran stopped to watch out of curiosity. It started as a civilised and orderly discussion about the nature of Jesus. One group proposed that Jesus, though he was one person, had two wills. He had one that was God's and another that was his human will. The other group proposed that he had only one will and that was God's. Each group put forward a speaker who explained their groups point of view. However, as the meeting went on, each group became more and more rowdy, and the meeting disintegrated into an unruly and ill-disciplined set of individual arguments. Aileran was confused and disturbed by this event. The growing anger and intolerance of each group towards the other seemed a long way from the kindness and generosity that he expected his fellow Christians to display. He could not help comparing the behaviour of these men of the church, who instructed the masses on how to behave with the actions of Father Gregor, Nicholas and Sophia in Thessaloniki. This arguing about who was right and who was wrong over a matter for which there was no proof one way or the other, seemed pointless to Aileran. To him it was like the Bishop of Rheims's behaviour; it seemed to be driven by the individual's egos and not their souls. For weeks afterwards he tried to make sense of what had taken place. Eventually, he concluded that both groups were convinced that they were basing their arguments on irrefutable facts, when, they were only based on strong opinions. Also, Aileran felt that for both groups it was more important to be right than it was to understand the other group's point of view. Furthermore, he felt that the subject of the discussion was irrelevant to most people outside the church and was simply a chosen battleground between two factions. He remembered similar disagreements taking place at Clonard and even then, they seemed to be driven by intellectual vanity and ego, not love and understanding.

Aileran stopped his reminiscing and looked ahead. Still no sign of any new pilgrims so he continued his recollections. A year ago, he himself was a pilgrim approaching the gates of Jerusalem. It had been a long journey, both physically and spiritually. To have finally arrived brought more a feeling of relief than of achievement. He had expected to feel elated as he had in Pavia at the tomb of Boethius; but instead he felt disappointingly flat. Over the days that followed he had wandered around the city feeling uncertain about what to do next. Most days he would find himself back at the gates watching people arrive at the city. In one of those moments, when he was not thinking about anything, the idea came to him that he should stop focussing on himself and instead look to see what he could be doing for others.

Weeks later

Caliph Umar had looked up from his desk as the guard on the door announced his visitors. Putting down his pen, he indicated to the guard to let them enter. Caliph Umar was a handsome man, with heavy eyebrows and piercing eyes. These, together with his magnificent moustache and beard could on another man appear fierce and intimidating but on Caliph Umar they did not because he also had the most welcoming smile which never left his face.

The group entered with Bishop Sophoronius at its head. He was followed by Rabbi Malachi ben Levi and a plainly dressed monk who the Caliph had never seen before. The Caliph moved towards them holding his hands out in greeting and as he spoke in fluent Latin his smile widened even further.

"Dear Sophoronius, it is wonderful to see you again." Caliph Umar had come to respect the Patriarch of Jerusalem. They had met when negotiating the surrender of the city of Jerusalem earlier that year and the Caliph had discovered during those negotiations that Sophoronius was a wise, kindly man who cared about all the people of Jerusalem, not just his flock. The bishop's honesty and integrity had been a major reason that the resulting agreement had avoided any damage or harm coming to the City of Jerusalem or its inhabitants. The bishop had not let the fact that he and the city were in the process of being conquered prevent him asserting what he felt was fair and reasonable.

The Caliph turned his attention to Rabbi Levi who bowed his head in respect.

"Welcome Rabbi Levi, again it is wonderful to see you too! I hope all is well with you and your people?"

Rabbi Levi was much shorter than both the Caliph and the Bishop. He was a very neat and tidy man with his hair shoulder length and with a beard which was freshly trimmed. If people remembered the Caliph for his welcoming smile and Bishop Sophoronius for his quiet unassuming manner, then they remembered the Rabbi's eyes with their sparkling twinkle. He always looked as if he had just thought of something amusing.

The Rabbi replied.

"Your Excellency, both I and my people are still in a state of euphoria and gratitude for your recent and most generous gift.

To be allowed to worship at the holy sites in the city, for the first time in 500 years, is truly wonderful!"

The Caliph seemed embarrassed to be spoken of in this way. Still smiling, as always, he spoke.

"Rabbi Levi, thank you for kind words but I have only returned to you and your people a right which should never have been taken away by the Romans in the first place."

Now, the Caliph thought, time to find out who the third member of the group was. He looked first at the stranger and then turned back to Bishop Sophoronius and raised one eyebrow quizzically. The bishop stepped forward and introduced the monk.

"Your Excellency, please allow me to introduce to you Brother Aileran of Clonard. He has travelled on a pilgrimage to Jerusalem from Ireland, the edge of the known world. Brother Aileran has come to us with an intriguing idea which we would like to share with you and to get your permission for us to implement."

The monk bowed low and held himself still for a moment before returning to the upright. His face was lined and weathered; that is, the part of his face that showed between his wild red hair and his even wilder red beard. He wore a plain monk's tunic which was even more worn than his face but, like his face, was free of dirt.

The Caliph returned the monk's bow but only with a nod of his head.

"Welcome Brother Aileran. Please, will you all make yourselves comfortable over here." The Caliph led them to a low table surrounded by many cushions of amazing colours. As servants brought fruit and water for the visitors, the Caliph looked around the room as he had done many times before. The room was a large and imposing space with carved columns running around all sides. It was originally built by the Romans as the main reception room of their Praetorium. When the group had refreshed themselves the Caliph, still smiling, caught the eye of Bishop Sophoronius who began to speak.

"Your Excellency, thank you for agreeing to see us, especially as you do not know yet the reason for our visit. If I may, I would like to ask Brother Aileran to explain his idea to you."

The Caliph nodded his consent and Brother Aileran began talking.

"Your Excellency, since I have arrived here, I have seen how important Jerusalem has become as a pilgrimage destination for many faiths including Christians like myself and Bishop Sophoronius, Muslims like yourself and Jews such as Rabbi Ben Levi. On my journey from Ireland I have witnessed how dangerous and challenging it is for everyone travelling the pilgrimage routes. These routes are plagued by illness, bandits and merchants who prey on the vulnerability of all pilgrims. When many arrive here in Jerusalem, they are often unwell, penniless and in need of support. Currently they struggle to survive, with some dying, some forced to beg and a few turning to crime. They come here to this city with the goal of redeeming their souls only to endure suffering as if they have arrived in hell. My idea is that we establish a multi-faith hospital that would provide free support to all pilgrims who arrive in the City so that they can recover and prepare themselves for the journey home. The hospital could be manned by volunteers from each faith group and be paid for by charitable donations raised from the rich, local residents."

Caliph Umar scanned the faces of the group and could see clearly that they were in support of Brother Aileran's idea.

"Please tell me more, especially what it is that you want from me?"

Bishop Sophoronius spoke next.

"Your Excellency, we have found a building that could be used to house the hospital. It was originally a Synagogue used by the

City's Jewish community before the Romans expelled them. It was then used as a warehouse by merchants before falling into disuse. It has been abandoned and unused for most of the past fifty years. It would be ideal for our hospital. Please would you give us your permission to use it for this purpose. Also, it is central to Brother Aileran's idea for the hospital to be multi-faith and we wondered if you would be able to appoint one of your religious leaders to work with us and to act as a link with your Muslim community?"

A week later, Aileran stood waiting as Rabbi Ben Levi unlocked the old Synagogue door. Caliph Umar had happily given his approval to Aileran's plan. As the door swung open and let in the light, Aileran could see the dusty floor strewn with rubbish. Rabbi Ben Levi went ahead and started opening the shutters on the row of side windows. Suddenly Aileran could see the whole of the large room and his eyes were immediately drawn to the ceiling where, contained within a large dome, was a beautiful mosaic. It shone brightly in the sunlight and depicted a huge tree covered in thousands of leaves of many different colours. As Aileran stood there, enraptured by the wonderous mosaic, he felt himself lifted on a wave of euphoria again as he had done at the tomb of Boethius in Pavia. He felt surrounded by golden light and completely weightless. In that moment there was no future and no past, just this moment. In that instant he understood why he had come to Jerusalem and what he must do with the rest of his life. Before him depicted as a tree was the whole of humanity and each a leaf represented a person. He could see that even though some of the leaves were different in size, shape and colour, they were still all leaves on the same tree. He also realised that his purpose in life was to find a way to serve all humanity as best he could. Gradually, as before, he returned to the present. Rabbi Ben Levi was standing in front of him looking intently at the ceiling as well. Aileran could see tears in the Rabbi's eyes.

"My ancestors have told stories of this mosaic during our exclusion from the city, and I never thought I would be the first

Jew to see it after five hundred years. I had always thought that the storytellers were exaggerating its beauty, but I was wrong. If anything, they failed to do it justice."

At this point there was a noise at the entrance of the synagogue and a group of people spilled into the large domed room. They were a mix of the city's citizens, made up of all faiths. Aileran was fascinated to watch their reaction as they looked upwards towards the ceiling and saw the mosaic for the first time. The look of wonder on each of their faces was unanimous. Among the crowd was Bishop Sophoronius and Iman Ibrahim who had been appointed by Caliph Umar to act on behalf of the city's Muslim community. Like everyone else, they were captivated by the magnificence of the mosaic ceiling. After a moment or two, Rabbi Ben Levi began organising the work party and together they set about cleaning up the building ready for its new role as a hospital.

The following day, Aileran was summoned to the old praetorium for a meeting with Caliph Umar. The Caliph was sat at his desk as Aileran entered the room. Caliph Umar took a sip of water then spoke softly, with that ever-present smile on his face.

"Thank you, Brother Aileran for sparing the time to visit me again so soon after our first meeting."

Brother Aileran smiled back

"It is my pleasure Caliph Umar, though I can't for the life of me think what such a busy and important man as you wants from such an unimportant man as me."

The Caliph laughed loudly.

"Surely, we are all important in the eyes of God?"

"You have a point there Your Excellency, but I am still curious; please tell me what it is you want from me."

"Ha!" exploded the Caliph laughing again.

"It is just that. Curiosity. I have never met a Peregrini before and I am curious about you and what you believe in. I may be, as you say a busy man, but one should never be too busy to learn from others.

Aileran was not at all accustomed to talking about himself and he felt quite uncomfortable sitting there in front of this powerful leader of the Islamic religion and being asked to articulate his most inner thoughts.

Aileran gave Caliph Umar a brief history of his life and then, prompted by Caliph Umar, he described his journey from Clonard to Jerusalem.

Caliph Umar, smiling as ever, looked up towards the ceiling and sat there silently lost in his thoughts.

"I can see that this personal and individual approach to finding God has an appeal to strong willed people like yourself. Your nature and your circumstances have required you be self-sufficient and to find your own way through the world. Brother Aileran, may I ask you, do you think that the God you have found is the same God that the monks at your Abbey in Ireland have found or the Nun in Pavia that you mentioned or the congregation in Rome?"

Responding to this question caused Aileran some difficulty.

"I am not sure that I can give you a satisfactory answer. The problem is that I cannot really articulate what my God looks like, and I cannot really understand what other people's God looks like to them. My journey has led me to believe that I should strive to achieve purity of heart, to always be sincere and to behave with humility. I should be willing to forgive others, to show love towards everyone, especially my enemies, to show mercy, to be charitable in judgement, to show compassion to those in need and to be honest in words and deeds. I have been fortunate to see many others along the way who demonstrate similar beliefs. Equally, I have seen others who appear to worship the same God as the others but do not demonstrate these beliefs. For instance, the Bishop of Rheims, who seemed to use charity for his own aggrandisement or the Clergy who argued furiously over whether Jesus had the will of man, the will of God, or both."

Caliph Umar became very intent at this point.

"Our great Prophet Muhammed believed in exactly those behaviours and so do I. Our religion of Islam is based on those beliefs. It is also possible to see the same beliefs being followed in the Jewish religion. This conversation has prompted me to remember a story that my uncle used to tell me when I was a small boy. It concerned a cave deep in the mountains of Persia. One day it was discovered by three brothers who had become lost while out hunting. The entrance of the cave was small and difficult to pass through so the youngest and smallest brother squeezed through the entrance and disappeared. Shortly afterwards, he reappeared in a state of excitement. He explained that inside the cave there was light without any openings to the outside world, and this light was a colour he had never seen before. When his brothers asked him to describe it, he told them it was a purplish blue with a tinge of pink and yet at the same time neither of these colours. The two elder brothers could not image this colour and became frustrated, so the middle brother attempted to enter the cave and managed to eventually squeeze through. Again, after a short while he returned and having struggled to get back out again, he explained what he had seen. However, his description was entirely different to his younger brother's description. He described it as bluish green with a tinge of orange. This frustrated the elder brother even more, so much so that he made a supreme effort and squeezed into the cave. Sure enough, after a short while he returned and with help from his brothers he eventually struggled back out. His description was different again. To him the colour was a golden pale yellow with a tinge of white. The three brothers began arguing with each other to the point where they started fighting. Each believed that they and only they had seen the true colour. Fortunately, they stopped fighting before any of them were seriously hurt. They spent the next two weeks finding their way back home and arguing all the way. When they got back to their home city, they began telling their story to anyone who would listen. After a time, each one had built up a following of people who were for some reason convinced by that brother's description. Years later the city had become divided with its citizens each convinced that their chosen brother was right and the other brothers were wrong. Every now and again violence broke out between one faction and another and for evermore their city was divided on grounds of belief.

When he had finished telling me this story, my uncle explained that the problem with us human beings is that we have limited ability to comprehend the reality that surrounds us. We are limited to our five senses. Uncle was a wise man and he believed that none of the brothers was right because their senses were not capable of perceiving the true colour in the cave and also, none of them possessed the language to be able to describe what was before them. It was also his opinion that human beings find it difficult to accept this, so they become convinced that the limited perception they manage to achieve is the truth and that all other views are false. The problem is further exacerbated by our personal view of ourselves and our desire to be right; our need to convince others of our point of view and our inclination to resist being convinced otherwise.

Reality is what it is, but we, as human beings, insist it is as we perceive it and we confuse our strong opinions with fact."

Aileran's mind was racing with the implications of the Caliph's story. He had never been presented with this view of humanity before. But something bothered him.

"Your Excellency, may I ask you a question related to your story and your personal belief?"

Caliph Umar's smile grew larger as he spoke.

"Brother Aileran, I would be disappointed if you did not."

"Do you believe that there is only one God, in the way that there was only one colour in the cave mentioned in your uncle's story?"

"Yes, most definitely!"

"And do you believe that all religions, including your own, are like the brothers with the colours, seeing the same God but differently?"

"I do, which is why I try to treat them equally with respect."

"Your Excellency, please forgive me for asking this next question. If that is the case, why are you conquering with force those all around you and further?"

Caliph Umar looked at Aileran as if seeing him for the first time.

"Ah, that is a different matter. We do not conquer to impose our religion upon others. We allow them to continue to worship freely. This is the reason why I have allowed the Jewish community to return to Jerusalem to worship. This city is as important to their religion as it to Christians and us Muslims. When the Prophet Muhammed led us from Mecca to Medina, it was to protect his followers from attack by our neighbours. Eventually it became clear that to survive and more importantly, thrive we needed to gain ascendency over these neighbours who threatened us constantly. We raised an army and defeated them. Some of those we fought were killed, some chose to convert to our religion, and some chose to remain worshipping their own God. We will continue to protect ourselves and our religion this way. All conquered peoples are free to worship who they want if they do not try to stop us worshipping our God. I am a straight-forward man and my way to God is through the wisdom of my friend and mentor, the Prophet Muhammad. I will do whatever it takes to create a part of the world where those who seek God are allowed to do so in their own way whilst protecting my right to do so in my way."

Later when Aileran was back in the hospital staring, as he often did, up at the glorious mosaic above his head, he replayed the conversation with Caliph Umar over and over in his head. He studied the Tree with its leaves of different shapes, colours, and sizes but still part of the same tree and decided that he was different to the Caliph. Therefore, his was a different future. He would remain in Jerusalem and be a humble servant to all those arriving on pilgrimage, regardless of their religious beliefs. He could not protect or support those pilgrims along the way, but he could do so when they reached their destination.

Aileran stopped turning his thoughts over in his mind and returned to the present. He looked up from his stool and saw in the distance two more pilgrims approaching. He realised that he had used all his jugs of water on the earlier pilgrims and that he had none to give to these new arrivals, so he quickly made his way to the nearby well to fill them before rushing back, hoping to be in time to welcome the travellers. As he got back to his stool, he was relieved to find he had returned just as the two pilgrims were approaching close by. For the first time he really looked at the pair as they came towards him. The taller of the two was dressed in the robes of an Orthodox Christian monk and the other was dressed in what appeared to be sackcloth. Aileran suddenly realised that he knew them and that they were Father Gregory and Solomon, both of whom he had last seen on the road to Thessaloniki. He rushed forward to greet them.

Four days later Aileran was sitting in the square outside the Tree of Life hospital and was in deep conversation with Solomon and Father Gregor. Solomon had been determined to finish his pilgrimage as soon as he had recovered, and Father Gregor had decided to keep him company. When they had first arrived, they had insisted that once they had given prayers of thanks at their respective places of worship, they would assist Aileran with his daily activities. Now, at the end of another day they were all reflecting on their time together. Aileran had revealed to them that he no longer considered himself to be a Christian but a believer in one God, who was all Gods in one. He also explained that he felt the Tree of Life mosaic on the ceiling of the Hospital perfectly described that this God had created all humanity as if they were all leaves on a tree and it was wrong to differentiate between them on the grounds of religion, race, appearance, or politics. He had also explained that he intended to see out his days providing a welcome, support and comfort to all pilgrims of all faiths. Solomon and Father Gregor had been moved by Aileran's disclosure and whilst neither of them felt that they wanted to change religions they did feel that they wanted to help passing pilgrims of all faiths during their journey. Father Gregor decided to return to Thessaloniki and create a similar service for passing pilgrims. Solomon decided to return to Colonia and assist pilgrims there. They agreed to maintain links between each other using pilgrims to carry communications between themselves. They further decided to keep their connection informal and discrete, driven by the needs of the pilgrims. One final decision was made to use the Tree of Life mosaic as a symbol for their informal organisation.

Chapter 3

The Smell of Old Leather

London March 2017

"Ok Stevie, I obviously know your story and that you have approached us because you want to become a hostage negotiator for our organisation. As I tried to explain on the telephone our organisation does not work like that. We are very selective as to who we invite to work for us. We keep our work secret and avoid publicity. Most people have never heard of us. You would never have found out about us if you had not been rescued by Chris and you were only able to contact us because you are the daughter of the US Secretary of State and to be honest, it is only out of courtesy to you and your father that we have asked you here today. Our normal approach is to receive recommendations from one or more of our members and then assess the possible candidate. We research their background to evaluate their abilities and past actions. If, after that, we decide they are a potential recruit then we approach them and invite them for an interview. Stevie, from the little that we know about you, we would not have identified you as a potential negotiator. Why are you so set on becoming one?"

Stevie looked at the elderly woman sitting across the coffee table from her. Her appearance was quite ordinary except for her eyes. They were a steel-blue colour, and her gaze was laser-like and difficult to return. Stevie's inner voice warned her not to underestimate this lady, so she answered as honestly as she could.

"The answer is because I must. When Chris Smith came to my rescue, I was an immature brat who had never thought too much about anybody but herself. I truly did not know what I wanted from life because I never thought about anything other than my immediate gratification. The time I spent with Chris kept me sane. He told me about how he came to dedicate his life to saving others. He told me how "The Seeker of Purpose" book got him started on the road to becoming a negotiator for your organisation. Since that time, I have never stopped thinking about Chris and what he did for me and I want to do the same for someone else,"

The woman, Mrs Joan Spencer, maintained her intense stare as she spoke,

"You do know that it is quite a common reaction especially if the negotiator and rescuer is killed saving the captive". Her face showed no emotion as she continued.

"I expect that you also feel guilty for being the cause of his death".

Stevie could feel herself becoming annoyed at Joan Spencer's words, but she controlled her anger.

"Yes, I was aware that this is quite common which is why I have spent the past months wrestling with my feelings. When I first returned, my emotions were highly unstable. I had the deaths of Chris and the Swedish boy replaying repeatedly in my mind and yes at that stage I did have a feeling of guilt. I eventually, went to see a psychologist to have counselling. The outcome was that whilst, I feel incredibly saddened by Chris's death, I do not feel guilty. In addition, I am even more certain that I want to dedicate my life to saving others".

Stevie was pleased she had kept her anger out of her voice and had spoken as dispassionately as her interviewer. Again, Joan Spencer spoke almost coldly.

"Please explain how it is that you no longer feel guilty for being the cause of Chris's death.

Stevie remembered asking Chris how he felt about death during one of their conversations.

Chris had replied. "How do I feel about death? Well, I am not afraid to die. I have always accepted that one day I will die. What is important is that when I die, I have not wasted my life. I had no control over being born and I have accepted that I will probably have no control over when I will die. I may have some choice over how I die if I am lucky, but my real choices are around how I chose to spend my life. I can accept my death when it comes if I have used my life to help others. I will even be happy to die violently or unpleasantly if I am attempting to save someone else's life at the time. "

Stevie replied to Joan Spencer

"Because it was Chris's decision to risk his life to save mine and not my choice. I will always regret being so stupid as to put myself in the position of needing to be rescued. I will remain grateful to Chris for saving me. I will always be saddened by his death, but it was the result of his choice not mine."

"And why are you so certain that you want to be a hostage negotiator?"

Stevie momentarily closed her eyes and tried to recall the words that she had been practising ready for this question.

"I have been given a second life by Chris and I want to use it to save people's lives wherever and whenever I can. I made a foolish mistake and right now other people are also making similar mistakes and like me, they are putting their lives at stake. I feel strongly that I was spared death so that I can save these people and give them a second chance. It will have made my life worthwhile if they feel about me the way I feel about Chris."

"Even if, like Chris, you are killed doing it?"

Stevie could not control her anger at this point.

"Of course, if Chris could die for me then I can die for someone else if necessary."

Joan Spencer said nothing for a while.

"Stevie, you do realise that you are not at all like Chris. He was completely different in fact from most people. He needed to help others to feel alive and to give him a sense of purpose. The more he helped people in difficult situations, the more he needed the next situation to be even more challenging. I am sad to say it was almost inevitable that he would never retire and enjoy reaching an old age. Chris never wanted recognition or gratitude, he just needed to know that he had successfully helped or saved someone and then he was onto the next challenge. You do not strike me as being someone who needs to help others that much. You seem to me to be someone who thinks that they ought to help somebody in need. For you it is an obligation not a calling. Which is ok, there are many people like that in the organisation. I am one such person. The Tree of Life Organisation is about more than just negotiating hostage rescue and within it there are many ways of helping the needy and unfortunate. Stevie, I cannot in all honesty progress any further with this interview if you are set in your intention to emulate Chris. If you are willing to be open to alternative ways that you can assist others and if we are able to see you put your intentions into practise, then possibly we might still invite you to join us."

Stevie's anger boiled up inside her again but this time she succeeded in controlling it.

"I am sorry, but you are wrong about me. I do need to dedicate my life to helping others. I have given this a lot of thought and I cannot go back to just thinking about myself and ignore those in need. You are right in that I am fixed in my desire to emulate Chris and be a negotiator, but not because my thinking is distorted by his death during my rescue. It is because its impact is clear to see. I would have been dead if Chris had not rescued me and someone else will be alive if I succeed in rescuing them."

Joan Spencer stood up and walked over to the bookcase and took down a large leather-bound book and placed it on the table in front of Stevie.

Stevie recognised it straight away and she ran her fingertips over the cover to feel the embossing and then she picked the book up and smelt it. It was just as Chris had described. It had a smell of old leather chairs and musty bookshops. She looked up at Joan Spencer who was smiling for the first time.

"Would you like to take the book away to read? We can talk further if you want."

In Washington, George McMaster put down the briefing note that he had been reading and answered his personal cell phone. He could see that the caller was Stevie.

"Hi Stevie, how are you?"

"I am fine Dad. Is this a convenient time to call?"

"Yes, it is a good time. How did you get on?

Stevie had already decided to be open and honest with her father and use his experience to help her to make her decision about what to do next.

"A bit mixed really. They rejected the idea of my becoming a negotiator. They were not convinced that I wanted to do it for the right reasons. However, they have left the door open to my fulfilling some other role for them."

George McMaster smiled to himself at this news.

"How do you feel about that?"

This time it was Stevie's turn to smile. She was pleased that her father had not expressed his pleasure at hearing that he had got what he wanted and that she would not be placing herself in danger and risking death like Chris.

"Initially, I was disappointed, but the more I have thought about it the more I understand their decision. My strong desire to replace Chris may just be a psychological reaction to his being killed while saving me and it may be that, deep down, I feel responsible for his death. If that is even a possibility, then they cannot take a chance on placing me in tricky situation where my life and someone else's life are at risk. The thing is, Dad, something attracts me to the idea of doing something worthwhile for others. There is something about the Tree of Life organisation being independent and secretive that appeals to me."

George McMaster, in that moment, realised how much he loved his daughter and how much he still missed his wife.

"Have you had any thoughts about what that might mean in terms of what you do next?

"No, not really. I think I will keep talking to them for the present. They have given me some reading to do and then I am going to meet them again to see if there is a better way I can contribute. Is it alright if I stay on here in your apartment for another week or so?"

"Of course, stay for as long as you like. Let me know if I can be of any help and Stevie, I haven't said this enough in the past, but I love you."

"I love you too Dad. Perhaps when I get back, we could spend some time together and we can discuss my future in more depth then."

"It's a deal. Stay safe."

"Bye, Dad!"

Stevie put her mobile down and thought about her father and their conversation and realised that when they do get together she will need to talk about her mother and her sudden death. Stevie now understood that there was a lot of suppressed emotion in her, and probably in her father too, that they had never tackled.

She crossed the apartment on the embankment of the River Thames and stared out at the park beyond. There were people walking dogs, others jogging at various speeds and people sitting in groups chatting and enjoying each other's company. Taking her coffee, she sat down in her father's big comfortable chair. As she picked up the heavy leather-bound book from the low table, she could not stop herself thinking back to that hell hole in Aleppo. Carefully she opened the book and began to read "The Seeker of Purpose".

Chapter 4

More a Vague Intention

The book began with an introduction. This story takes place during a very dark time. It is a time of oppression, a time when the established order has been swept away by foreign invaders in a brutal and uncompromising manner. These invaders are only interested in power and wealth. They are not driven by some political or philosophical motive. They are driven by greed and the need to dominate. But what of the original inhabitants of this invaded land? Their King has been killed along with his closest supporters. Also killed, often brutally with extreme malice, has been anyone who has shown any sign of resistance, disapproval or resentment. The invasion took place four years ago and since then the Normans, as the invaders were known, have been relentlessly suppressing and eliminating any form of non-submission. If you were Anglo-Saxon at this time, you had limited choice, either you swore allegiance to the Normans or became an outlaw to be hunted and harried into remote and wild places. Most Anglo-Saxons tried to keep their heads down and go unnoticed if they could, rather than be required to make that choice.

The place where we begin this story is Maeldubesburg. It sits many miles west of Lunden, almost as far as the River Severn. It had been an important Anglo-Saxon town and had a well-established Abbey where King Athelstan had been buried. Like many other Saxon towns, it is now under the control of a Norman Lord. The town is now dominated by an imposing wooden tower built by the Normans next to the Abbey and guarding the western gate to the town. The tower stands over ten metres high and is made of solid timber. It is designed not only to provide protection for the Norman Lord and his band of warriors but to also remind the conquered that they are subject to the will of a martial power. Maeldubesburg itself sits on a natural defensive feature, an outcrop of rock overlooking the surrounding countryside and therefore the tower is visible from miles around. At the top of the tower, we find a boy, his name is Aelfgar. It is late at night. He sits there in the dark with his back against the battlements. His mind is turning over the day's events. The day had been a catastrophe. For years he had been treading a fine line between resisting his uncle's demands and provoking his uncle's anger. Today he had stepped over the line and his uncle had nearly killed him.

What had caused this to happen? Well to understand this it is necessary to understand Aelfgar's background and that of his uncle. Let us start with Aelfgar. Aelfgar was born in the year of 1056. His father, Aethelwulf Angarson was a King's Thegn, and his mother Beatrice de Beauville was the daughter of a Norman Lord. For different reasons neither were directly involved in Aelfgar's upbringing. During the first decade of his life his father was frequently away either fighting or on the King's service until eventually he never returned. His mother, always pious became more and more withdrawn into prayer. In Aethelwulf's absence his younger brother Sigewulf looked after the King's land and the boy's upbringing. Sigewulf and his wife Aemma had no children of their own and had all but adopted Aelfgar as their son. Aelfgar had loved his uncle Sigewulf and his aunt Aemma and if asked he would have said that his life was good. Every now and then his father would appear and spend time with Aelfgar, and this was always exciting. His father was a hero who carried out special duties for King Edward and was a charismatic man who always made his son feel special. When Aethelwulf was away, Sigewulf and Aemma, provided the boy with stability and made sure he studied and developed into a worthy Saxon boy. He would see his mother regularly because, though she took no responsibility for his upbringing, she wanted him to be as much Norman as Anglo-Saxon. For her this meant being able to speak French, to worship God and attend mass every day. If left to his own devices Aelfgar would have chosen to be completely Anglo-Saxon like his father, his uncle Sigewulf and his aunt Aemma. However, Aelfgar took the line of least resistance and even though he thought of himself as Anglo-Saxon he went along with his mother's wishes becoming fluent in both French and Latin. His relationship with his mother was strange because he could not remember any time in his life when she has shown him any affection let alone had hugged him. He was reasonably fond of his mother, but he did not love her in the way he loved his Aunt Aemma. As with many boys of his age he did not think about his life too much if at all. He certainly gave no thought to the future. He had no real friends but at the same time he had no enemies either. Life carried on comfortably until he was about 10 years old when it started to go wrong. In January 1066, the King died. Edward had been King for 24 years and had left no children. This brought uncertainty and then the Normans under William of Normandy invaded. Immediately, Aelfgar's Norman uncle, Ralf de Beauville, arrived in Maeldubesburg with a small army of Norman soldiers and seized the town and surrounding countryside in the name of William of Normandy. Ralf had always held a grudge against his sister Beatrice for marrying an Anglo-Saxon and immediately banished her to a monastery. He had hoped to have the opportunity to kill Aethelwulf but had to satisfy himself with killing Sigewulf instead. Aelfgar was spared, not out of mercy but because the boy could be useful to him in controlling the newly acquired Saxon territory. Ralf insisted that Aelfgar was now his ward and would be brought up as a Norman. Aelfgar had resisted this, and it was this resistance that led to today's unpleasant and near fatal events. Today was Aelfgar's 14th birthday and Ralf demanded that Aelfgar now take the name Simon de Beauville, cut off his long blond hair and adopt the Norman tonsured style of haircut. He was then to swear allegiance to Ralf and become his vassal. In a moment of defiance Aelfgar angrily refused. Ralf responded with matching anger, drew his sword and was about to bring it down on Aelfgar's head when he regained control of himself but still pointing his sword at the boy gave him until dawn to change his mind or face the consequences.

Aelfgar now sat there at the top of the tower. His mind was churning, reliving the events of the day.

He felt lost and alone, scared about what his uncle might do. Since his uncle Sigewulf had died and his aunt Aemma had disappeared he had no-one to talk to. Even going to visit his mother, with whom he had never had a real conversation, was out of the question. His Uncle Ralf kept Aelfgar close to him and cut off all contact with Aelfgar's previous Anglo-Saxon life. At first Aelfgar clung to the idea that his father would return and kill Ralf and make things right again, but his father never came, and hope turned into anger. Where was his father? Why had he abandoned Aelfgar? Recently, Aelfgar's anger had turned into worry, fuelled by his uncle Ralf's insistence that he had heard that Aethelwulf had died in Sicily. What confused Aelfgar was that, despite his uncle's confidence that Aethelwulf was dead, he felt somewhere deep inside himself that this was not true. Aelfgar was also angry with himself because he felt that he should have tried to kill his uncle in revenge for the murder of Sigewulf. Aelfgar wished that he was a hero, like his father who could take on anyone and defeat them. But he knew that he was like his late uncle Sigewulf, more concerned with maintaining peace than starting a fight. He had hoped that if he went along with Ralf's demands he would be able to influence Ralf to the benefit of the people of Maeldubesburg. He soon found out that his uncle was only influenced by greed and the accumulation of power. To give in to Ralf meant you had to do what he said, to stand up to him meant you had to be prepared to kill or be killed.

Aelfgar felt completely frustrated and unable to deal with this terrible conundrum. The more he thought about it the more confused he became. Then, after hours of turmoil out of nowhere, a thought began to crystallise. Slowly it became clearer and clearer. It was that he only had three options. Either to capitulate to his uncle's will; to face his uncle down defiantly and almost certainly die; or to run away from all that he had ever known. None of these were an appealing choice but something deep down inside him was telling him to run away. Run away to what; where to go; how to survive? Aelfgar had never left Maeldubesburg or the surrounding area and the thought of doing so scared him. He stood up and kicked the wooden wall of the keep. What should he do? How to decide? Through his anger Aelfgar realised that the voice deep inside was still saying "Run away, stop thinking and just do it!" So Aelfgar made himself calm down and thought "If I am going to run away that will not be an easy thing to do. Uncle Ralf will have worked out that my running away could be a possibility and will be ready to prevent it". Aelfgar recognised that to escape he needed to outthink his uncle and that was going to be a challenge. "Firstly, I need to gain some more time while I look for an opportunity to escape" he thought to himself. So, after hours of sitting up on the battlements, Aelfgar descended into the great hall.

Sitting at the head table surrounded by his Norman henchmen sat the boy's uncle, drinking wine and picking at his food. He looked up as the boy entered.

"Ah there you are, you pig-headed little whelp. Have you come to your senses yet"? Instinct told Aelfgar not to be confrontational. He replied in a subdued voice.

"I am trying to, uncle, but my mind is still confused about what I should do".

"For God's sake" roared his uncle. "It is bloody obvious what you should do. Put aside your Saxon pride and become my vassal".

The boy suddenly had an idea of how he could get outside of the castle. Keeping his voice subdued he said

"I know Uncle, I want to, but something is holding me back. Perhaps if I went to the Abbey and prayed to God, he will help me find a way to overcome my reticence".

"Do what you bloody like, boy! Just be sure to agree to my wishes in the morning!" Then, turning to one of his companions, he bellowed.

"Odo, go with the boy to the Abbey and make sure that you keep an eye on him". The sergeant-at-arms stood up, shooting Aelfgar an irritated look as he came towards the boy.

"By God, you are more trouble than you are worth. If it were up to me, I would have killed you along with your snivelling Saxon uncle. Come on, let us get going."

As they left the keep on their way to the Abbey, the boy thought back to the time four years ago when his Norman uncle had killed his Uncle Sigewulf.

A few days before this murder a band of Saxon warriors on the way back home to Gleawanceaster had brought the news that King Harald had been killed during a battle on the south coast. They told how the invading Norman army had defeated the Saxon army and was heading towards Lunden to claim the Crown. So, when on the morning of the murder a young farm boy, breathless from running, had come into the main hall and informed Sigewulf that a small army was approaching Maeldubesburg, everyone was taken by surprise. Sigewulf gathered the town council and went to the south gate to meet this army. Aelfgar was curious to see what would happen, so he had joined the tail of the group as they hurried towards the gate and had stood silently at the back as the soldiers came galloping towards them. They were Normans. A formidable sight dressed in long chain mail tunics, wearing helmets and riding in perfect formation with lances pointing straight up towards the sky. They had come to a sudden halt a short distance from the awaiting group. Their horses complained but executed the stop with precision. One of the Normans, the only one without a lance, had dismounted and stepped forward.

"I am Ralf de Beauville, I am the elder brother of your Lady Beatrice, and I am now your Lord and Master. Harald is dead, William is now King, and I will be governing this territory in his name". His voice was loud but not strained, fierce but controlled and his stare was withering. He looked at the group before him.

"I have heard that my brother-in-law Aethelwulf is away somewhere on the old King's business. I understand that my sister in not interested in this world only the next. I believe that Aethelwulf's brother has been acting on his behalf and running things in his absence. Which one of you is Sigewulf?" He stood looking directly at the group with one hand on his sword and with his legs astride ready for action. Sigewulf, recognising his name, stepped forward slowly and replied in Anglo-Saxon.

"I am Sigewulf, Thegn in my brother's absence. I do not understand you as I do not speak French. I will find my nephew and ask him to translate our words".

Ralf de Beauville was annoyed as he in turn could not understand Sigewulf.

Aelfgar, on hearing Sigewulf's words, moved reluctantly forward through the men of the town council and stood beside his uncle Sigewulf.

"Aelfgar, my boy, introduce yourself to this Norman and tell him that you will translate our words so that we can understand each other."

"Yes, Uncle but I am scared. "

"Aelfgar, remember whose son you are and that you are representing every Saxon in Maeldubesburg. Hold yourself with pride and translate our words exactly."

Aelfgar had looked up at his Norman uncle and spoke in French.

"I am Aelfgar, son of Aethelwulf, nephew of Sigewulf and son of your sister Beatrice. My uncle Sigewulf has commanded me to act as translator so you may both understand each other."

Ralf de Beauville had looked him up and down.

"Well, well, well. So, my sister did not forget that she was Norman. You may look like a Saxon, but you certainly sound like a Norman. Tell Sigewulf that I agree to your translating our words and then tell him what I said when I arrived. And Aelfgar, make sure you translate our words accurately as all your lives depend upon it."

Aelfgar had informed his uncle Sigewulf of Ralf de Beauville's response and then translated the Norman's first words.

Sigewulf had looked at the boy as he translated and when Aelfgar had finished he spoke to Aelfgar in a quiet and calm way.

"Aelfgar, listen very carefully. I am going to reply to this Norman bastard in a way that he will not like. You must translate not just my words but my feelings. Whatever follows you must not get involved. You must maintain the neutral position of being a translator. Do you understand?"

Ralf de Beauville was becoming angry at this side conversation that he could not understand. He felt he was losing control.

"Boy, what are you talking about? Translate your uncle's words for me immediately."

"He was instructing me as you did to translate his words accurately and stressing the importance of my doing so. My uncle has a reply for you which I will translate as soon as he has finished giving it."

"Well, get on with it" Ralf shouted at Sigewulf.

Sigewulf had taken a step forward to stand directly in front of Ralf de Beauville. He held himself in a relaxed and confident way. He spoke calmly with a dignified manner.

"As I have already said, I am the Thegn of this area in the absence of my brother Aethelwulf until he returns or is proven dead. I come from a long line of Saxon warriors all of whom would haunt me in the afterlife if I were to just submit and hand Maeldubesburg to you. Therefore, I challenge you to mortal combat. If you win, then the town and surrounding villages will accept you as their new lord. If I win, your soldiers will ride away and leave us alone". Sigewulf stopped and maintained his steady stare into Ralf de Beauville's eyes.

Aelfgar, remembering Sigewulf's instructions had translated this reply into French maintaining the calm dignity of Sigewulf's original delivery. He had not finished his translation when Ralf reacted. He had just translated the challenge to mortal combat when Ralf drew his dagger and plunged it into Sigewulf's chest. As he did so his soldiers kicked their horses into action and formed a semi-circle around the townspeople with their lances at the ready. Sigewulf lay dead on the floor and Ralf shouted to Aelfgar to tell this rabble that unless they dropped their weapons on the floor then they would be joining Sigewulf in the afterlife.

At this point, the boy's reverie is broken by shouting coming from outside the Hog's Head inn which is between the castle and the abbey. Odo's mates are calling him to enjoy a drink with them.

"Odo!" one of them shouts. "Where are you going? Come and join us for a drink." Odo scowled at the soldier and replied.

"I am taking this snivelling Saxon pain in the arse to the abbey on Lord Ralf's orders and I must keep an eye on him. Otherwise I would join you."

The soldier stood up and made room for Odo.

"Odo! You can sit here. You can see the Abbey doors from here. He cannot leave without you seeing him. Come on, we are just beginning a new game of dice!"

Odo was torn. To disobey Lord Ralf could be fatal but he usually won at dice and this boy was not worth passing up this opportunity. Turning to Aelfgar, he spoke menacingly.

"Look boy, I am going to be sitting here watching the abbey. If you try to leave, I will see you and I will give you a beating so severe you may not survive it. Do you understand?"

Aelfgar grunted that he did.

"Remember that when you are finished you should open the door to the Abbey and stand and wait for me to collect you. Do not move from the doorway, even if I do not come straight away. I will be watching and will be angry if you do not do what I have told you."

With that Odo took the boy into the abbey and having checked that all other doors were locked, left to join his friends.

Aelfgar waited and after checking that all the other doors were in fact locked and that there was no other way out of the abbey, he carefully eased the main door open enough to look across to the inn. There sitting opposite him was Odo, his attention completely on the dice game in front of him. Aelfgar closed the door and reflected that whilst he had managed to get out of the castle, he was no nearer to escaping.

Outside Odo was on a winning streak and enjoying another jug of ale. He looked up regularly and checked the abbey doorway. This time when he looked up, he saw a monk approaching the abbey with an armful of candles to make ready for first Mass. Odo watched as the monk entered the abbey to ensure the boy did not slip out. The door shut and everything was quiet except for the rowdy banter around the table. Odo returned his attention to the dice game. A little while afterwards the monk left the abbey and returned to the dormitory. Odo's luck took a reversal and in no time he had lost all the money he had won earlier and a bit more. He was in a foul mood when he went over to the abbey to check on the boy. Opening the door, the first thing he saw was a pile of candles scattered over the floor. The next thing he saw was a naked monk bound and gagged on the nearby pew. Odo drew his sword and rushed outside towards the dormitory, leaving the monk still bound, gagged and naked.

Aelfgar by now was a mile away, making his way along the river Afon towards Scorranstan due west of Maeldubesburg. He was no longer dressed as a monk, having kept his own clothes on under the monk's habit. He was in a small punt pushing himself away from Maeldubesburg. He had managed to steal the boat unnoticed down by the old mill on the edge of Maeldubesburg. It would be inaccurate to say that he had a plan, more a vague intention. Aelfgar had nothing with him other than the clothes he was wearing and his dagger. He had decided to make his way to the nunnery at Wickselm which was close by the River Severn and was where his mother lived, to see if he could obtain her help to get some food, money and even a horse. As he was approaching the village of Scorranstan the river came close to the road from Maeldubesburg. There he heard galloping horses and, shortly afterwards a troop of Norman soldiers passed him in the dark heading in his direction of travel. Aelfgar decided it would be wise to avoid Scorranstan and he abandoned his punt and left the river at this point to set off across country.

After a few hours of hard walking Aelfgar felt the day catch up with him. All the emotional turmoil and physical stress had taken its toll and he desperately needed to rest so he found a secluded spot deep in a wood and went to sleep. Before long he started to dream. He quite often had vivid dreams. Usually, they made no sense to him when he awoke. In this dream the sun was coming up over the horizon and beginning to shine on him. He was standing in the middle of a battlefield, clothed in chain mail with a heavy helmet on his head, holding his sword in front of him. Around him on the ground were the bodies of men dressed in strange uniforms. He felt very weary and cold. There was a shield standing upright in front of him, wedged into the ground. Aelfgar tried to walk around it to see what was on the front, but his legs would not work. He concentrated all his will on trying to move and eventually he managed to edge his way around. It was like wading through thick mud and took extraordinary effort to succeed. When he was eventually able to see the front of the shield, he was shocked to see it was not his, but his father's coat of arms emblazoned there. Aelfgar had seen it many times during his father's visits. It was a red background with a black bear looking fierce and wielding a battle axe. At that same moment, there was a bright flash and he felt as if he was tumbling through the air. Suddenly he was standing in a forest clearing filled with bright sunshine and birdsong. It was so different from a moment ago. Before, he was cold, he was now warm. Where before there was death now there was life. In front of him was a large tree and it seemed to be on fire. Every branch was covered in tiny flames glowing red, but the flames did not seem to be consuming the tree. They seemed more as if they were decorating it.

A movement below the tree caught Aelfgar's eye and when he looked, he saw an elderly woman dressed in dark green robes. Her long hair was blowing in a breeze, and she was holding out her arms towards Aelfgar. It was as if she was beckoning him to come to her. She spoke but he could not understand her words. Aelfgar leant forward to hear her better. Suddenly he was awake and for a moment could not remember where he was. He became aware of a pain where the bark of the tree was pressing against his back. He could also feel the damp seeping into his clothing. Through the trees he could see that the sun had risen. Gradually, he began to remember where he was and what had led up to his being here. He realised that he was now in uncharted territory with no-one to rely on but himself. He felt cold and hungry and very alone. He started to walk and as he did, he recalled his dream. Or was it two dreams? What did it mean? He shook his head to clear his mind and to begin the descent towards the River Severn. After a while, the ferns got thicker, and he frequently stumbled and nearly fell. It seemed to Aelfgar that he had been descending through the trees forever. His mind was completely preoccupied with the dream of his father's shield, the woman and the flame tree when he approached the edge of the wood above the nunnery. He found a footpath leading towards the front gate and was just about to step out from the shade when he was startled by a hand on his shoulder. A low gentle voice said.

"I wouldn't go down there if I were you, Aelfgar".

The boy turned and drew his knife. Standing before him was a monk.

"Who the bloody hell are you? How come you know my name?" demanded Aelfgar.

"I am Father Dominic and I have been sent by your mother to tell you that two of your uncle's men are waiting for you outside the gatehouse of the nunnery".

"Well, Father Dominic" said Aelfgar, still angry.

"You gave me one hell of a shock. How on earth did you get so close without me hearing you?"

The old monk chuckled as he looked Aelfgar straight in the eye.

"I haven't always been a monk and it seems some of my old skills haven't deserted me. Now we must move fast before your uncle's men get tired of waiting and decide to come looking for you." He turned and started back the way Aelfgar had come. Aelfgar felt his anger suddenly flare up. He was not sure why. He knew the monk was only trying to help him, but Aelfgar resented being told what to do. This sudden overwhelming rage was probably as much a reaction to the past twenty-four hours as to anything the monk had done.

"Wait!" called Aelfgar, "I am going nowhere! I need food and water. I have not eaten anything since yesterday." It was now Father Dominic's turn to be angry.

"Be quiet, you young fool, or they will hear you. I have food and water waiting for us down by the water's edge. Now, in the name of the Holy Mother, come along." As quickly as it had flared up, Aelfgar's anger died away, and he followed the monk quietly towards the river.

They soon came to a small inlet where in amongst the reeds a small boat lay hidden. Aelfgar climbed in and just as Father Dominic was about to join him two Norman soldiers burst through the bushes and rushed towards them. With amazing speed Father Dominic picked up one of the oars and attacked the leading soldier. The Norman raised his sword to strike at Father Dominic who suddenly lunged forward with all the force

74

he could muster. The tip of the oar blade went under the soldier's nose guard and struck him just beneath his nose and he fell to the ground unconscious. Father Dominic regained his balance and was just turning to face the second attacker when the blade of the man's sword struck him forcefully in his side. Father Dominic screamed in agony and fell onto one knee. The Norman then stepped forward and raised his sword to strike Father Dominic a fatal blow. Before he could deliver it, Aelfgar had leapt from the boat over Father Dominic and stabbed the soldier through the eye, straight into his brain, killing him. Aelfgar stood there, frozen. Even though he had been trained in fighting skills, this was the first person he had killed. He felt numb and paralysed. Father Dominic managed to gain his attention.

"Aelfgar, help me get into the boat and then push us off into the centre of the stream." Aelfgar came to his senses and helped Father Dominic, who obviously was badly injured, into the boat. After retrieving the oar that Father Dominic had used, he then waded in the water, pushed the boat forward into the flow and scrambled aboard. Father Dominic looked ashen as he gave Aelfgar instructions.

"Row us out of the inlet and into the middle of the river so that the ebb tide can carry us away." Aelfgar was uncertain what to do.

"But what about your injuries, we should take a look at them and see what we can do?" Father Dominic shook his head irritably.

"We can do that when we are riding the tide downstream. Keep rowing."

So Aelfgar rowed with all his might. He was thankful for his strong Anglo-Saxon build and that he was starting to become a young man and leave childhood behind. As he rowed, he relived the attack by his uncle's men and marvelled at how well Father Dominic had fought. Had Father Dominic, not reacted the way he did, then for certain Aelfgar would now be on his way back to Maeldubesburg to face the wrath of his uncle. Thinking about it, Aelfgar wondered why Father Dominic had fought the two

Normans when he could have just handed him over. Aelfgar then started to think about the fact that he had killed a man. Strangely he did not feel guilty perhaps because he did it to save Father Dominic's life. He did not, however, feel that taking the man's life was something to be proud about. On balance he would have preferred not to have killed him if he had had the choice. This led him to reflect on the fact that he was not at all like his father who never seem be bothered about slaying his enemies. It suddenly occurred to Aelfgar that maybe he was not destined to follow in his father's footsteps as he had always assumed.

Father Dominic's voice broke the boy's reverie. It sounded very weak.

"Aelfgar, my boy, you can stop rowing for a moment. I can feel the tide carrying us down river. Come close, I have something I need to tell you, whilst I have the strength. You must keep to the very centre of the river as there are many rocks close into shore. In about two hours, you will feel the tide begin to ease before turning. When you feel that happen, you must head for the shore on the north bank. There you should see a beacon burning in the distance. This will be the guiding beacon at the entrance to the River Taff. You must head for the light. Once you reach the entrance to the river you should pull up onto the west bank. You then need to destroy the boat and look for an ancient stone cross at the start of a footpath heading north toward LLandaff. Do not take this path but strike out westwards up the valley towards the high ground. The valley will head west for about a mile and then turn north and upwards to an ancient forest on the top of a high hill. Someone will be waiting for you there."

Aelfgar was puzzled

"What about you, you talk as if you will not be there?"

"Aelfgar, before I became a monk, I was a warrior. I have seen many men wounded by sword blows and I know that I am dying. I will not last much longer. Now please listen as I still have important things to tell you whilst I can. I want you to reach into my pouch where you will find something I want you to have. Please get it out and open it."

Aelfgar did as he was instructed. He opened Father Dominic's pouch and found a small package. He untied the cord and unwrapped the soft leather to discover a small brass brooch, the kind used to fasten a cloak. In the moonlight Aelfgar could see that there was some decoration on the front of the brooch.

"Listen very carefully to what I have to say next because your life could depend on you remembering it well. By running away, you have started on a perilous journey which is taking you away from everything you have ever known. You will need to dig deep inside yourself to survive but you need not be alone. There are many people who can and will help you if they are able." Father stopped speaking and closed his eyes, then with great effort opened them again and continued.

"There is so much I need to tell you and I can feel that I have only a little time left. Wherever you go on your journey you should look out for a sign that help is available. It could be a flag, a carving, or badge, or brooch or appear in many other forms. You will know it because it will be the same sign as on that brooch. You must always keep it safe, because without it no-one will know to help you. When you see the sign on your journey wear the brooch on your chest where it is visible. It is important that you wear it upside down as this is the signal that you need help. If you wear it the right way up, you will be ignored. Do you understand, Aelfgar?"

"Yes, Father Dominic, but who are these people and what is this all about?"

"I am sorry Aelfgar, but I don't have time to answer your questions. I will have to leave that to others. Now, if you wear your brooch upside down then you will eventually be approached by someone. This person could be anyone, but you will know them because they will speak to you in Latin and will ask you the following question. They will say "I am looking for the house of the Lord. Can you help me?" and you must reply in

Latin exactly as I say. You must say "I am a stranger here myself. I am looking for a place to rest." Your reply will let them know you are not an impostor who has found or stolen your brooch. You will know they are genuine because they will now say to you "There are places to rest in the house of the Lord" to which you should reply "Well, perhaps we can look together" and then they will say finally "Yes, let us start by looking down this way" and they will take you to somewhere safe where you will be able to talk openly. "

"Now tell me honestly Aelfgar, will you be able to remember all that I have said word for word?" Father Dominic lifted his head, so he could see Aelfgar's face. Aelfgar instinctively moved closer before he replied.

"Yes, I will remember." Father Dominic winced as a sharp pain shot through his body. Barely audible he started to speak again.

"Aelfgar, never tell anyone at all what I have just told you." With that he dropped his head and lay staring at the stars. It was only the slight rise and fall of his chest that indicated that he was still alive.

Aelfgar held the brooch tightly in his hand; he had so many questions he needed to ask. Father Dominic started to cough and moan. After a short while he stopped and turning to Aelfgar he spoke.

"Aelfgar, I am close to death and there is one more thing I need you to do. When I am dead you must tip my body into the river, so it is not found when you abandon the boat. Promise you will do this for me." Aelfgar was shocked and he grabbed Father Dominic's hand.

"I can't do that. I could get help or bury you myself." Father Dominic returned his grip with surprising strength.

"No, I will already be with God and my body will decompose either way on land or in the sea. Your uncle will keep searching for you and my body would be a clue to where you went ashore. It is best my way. Now promise me!"

Aelfgar looked at the monk he had only known for a few hours but to whom he owed so much. He could not deny Father Dominic his dying wish and said,

"I promise". Father Dominic was not satisfied.

"Aelfgar, I want you to swear on something dear to you, so I know you will carry out my wishes". Reluctantly Aelfgar swore an oath.

"I swear on the memory of my father that I will do as you say."

As he spoke Aelfgar noticed a smile appear of Father Dominic's face.

"Ah, your father, he is a great man and if you are lucky, you may see him again."

Aelfgar was confused "What do you mean, see him again?" but he never got an answer because Father Dominic had already died.

Stevie put down the book for a moment and remembered herself running away to Syria and the mixture of fear and exhilaration that she had felt. At that time, she had despised her father. When she was captured and held hostage, and in fear for her life, she had blamed her father for the situation. She now realised that by running away and making her own decisions, she had been solely responsible for her actions and that no one else was to blame. Furthermore, she could now see how misguided and impetuous she had been. After the sudden death of her mother, all she could think about was herself and how much she was hurting. She thought her father did not care about her and with twisted logic she had put herself in danger, as a form of revenge. It had never occurred to her that her father might be hurting too and that his way of dealing with it was to bury himself in his work.

Returning her mind to the present, she could feel an affinity with Aelfgar and the journey he was taking with no idea of how it would all end. She returned to the book and continued reading.

Chapter 5

Safe Haven

Aelfgar lay hidden in the bracken halfway up the valley side overlooking the ancient stone cross. He had been there since his arrival a few hours earlier. He had spent the time thinking about his situation and the many questions swirling around in his head. He could feel his uncle's fury even though he was many miles from Maeldubesburg. He knew his uncle would take his absconding as a personal insult and would be determined to get his revenge on his nephew. He would never stop looking for him. His plans to use Aelfgar as an example to other Anglo-Saxons of accepting and adopting a Norman way of life were now ruined and in fact Aelfgar had now become an example of rejecting such acceptance. Aelfgar also thought a lot about Father Dominic. Who exactly was he and why had he chosen to fight the two Norman soldiers and not just hand Aelfgar over to them? Where was Father Dominic sending him and who was he supposed to be meeting in the ancient forest? Why had Father Dominic given him the brooch and why the need for secret codes? Aelfgar had spent a long time studying the brooch. On the front there was an engraving that depicted a tree in full leaf. On the ground beneath the tree lay a pile of fallen leaves. What did it mean? In fact, was there any significance in the detail of this decoration. Aelfgar also remembered the dreams he had in the wood. What could they mean?

Most puzzling of all, and causing Aelfgar the most confusion, was what had Father Dominic meant by saying "if you are lucky, you may see him again". Did that mean his father was still alive? If so, why had he not been in contact? Did he mean that Aelfgar might find his grave? In that case why did he say, "He is a great man" and not "he was a great man?"

Aelfgar had got to a point where he could no longer think clearly. He was physically and emotionally drained. He was extremely hungry as the food that Father Dominic had promised was still stashed away by the river at Wickselm. There was no point in staying where he was any longer, so he decided to move on. He carefully parted the fronds of the bracken and studied the valley below him. There was nobody in sight, so he descended to the valley floor. He started walking up the valley away from the stone cross heading for the high ground on the horizon. After about a mile the valley turned north, as Father Dominic had predicted and high on the hill ahead, he could make out a dense and forbidding forest. After a steep climb he came to the edge of the forest. He could see no sign of anyone waiting for him. He stopped and scanned the trees. Something caught his attention far over to the left. It was a patch of colour, red, and when he turned and looked more closely, he was amazed to see a tree that seemed to be on fire, just like in his dream. He also realised that, as in his dream, there was also bright sunshine and the sound of birds singing. He walked towards the tree and as he came closer, he could see that the tree was not covered in tiny flames as in his dream but bright red berries smothering a Rowan tree. He gave a little laugh as he realised this. "Fool! Of course, trees do not bear flames in real life. A dream is a dream and not real life," he said to himself out loud. Aelfgar was still chuckling to himself at his foolishness when a figure stepped out from behind the Rowan tree.

"Welcome Aelfgar" said an elderly woman dressed in green robes.

"Welcome to the ancient forest of Morgannwg." For the second time in less than twelve hours Aelfgar was stopped in his tracks by a stranger that knew his name. Who was this woman and why had she appeared in his dreams? Exhausted as he was, all Aelfgar could do was stand and stare with his mouth wide open. The elderly woman spoke again.

"Aelfgar, you probably do not recognise me, but I am your grandmother. Your father is my son and people call me Ffraid the Seer or Ffraid of the Ancient Woods. I have been waiting for you."

Aelfgar was already confused and puzzled before this encounter and reacted angrily.

"I don't have a grandmother. I have never heard of you. No-one has ever mentioned a grandmother to me. Why do you say you are my grandmother?"" The elderly woman smiled lovingly as she held her finger gently to her lips.

"Aelfgar, that and the many other questions you have will take some time to answer. Let us go to my home, which is nearby, where you can rest while I prepare some food for you. Once you have eaten, I will try to answer all your questions as best I can." She then turned and started along a path leading deep into the woods.

Aelfgar stayed rooted to the spot. Nothing made sense. One moment he is in Maeldubesburg trying to escape his uncle's wrath, then he is on the shore of the River Severn killing a Norman soldier and now he is in an ancient forest with a stranger who says that she is his grandmother. He was not moving until he was given some answers. The elderly woman returned to his side and smiled patiently. She gently placed her hand on his arm and spoke in a quiet, calm voice.

"Aelfgar, please trust me. I do not wish you any harm. Please follow me. It is not far." Aelfgar's inner tension eased a little bit, but he still did not move. Looking directly into the eyes of this woman who claimed to be his grandmother he said.

"Tell me this, how did you know I was coming to this spot and how did Father Dominic know you would be waiting?" Ffraid sensed that if she did not give the boy a proper answer he would stubbornly stay put.

"Aelfgar I will answer those questions but first I want you to answer a question of mine. On your journey here did you have any dreams?"

Aelfgar was disturbed. How did this woman know that he had had those dreams? Nothing seemed to make sense. He felt himself becoming agitated again and he could not stop himself blurting out aggressively "Yes, and in one of them I saw you calling to me from this spot. I do not understand it. How is it possible?

Ffraid remained calm and replied

"I do not know how it is possible, but I have, and it seems you have, a gift for seeing things across time and space. Anyway, I became aware of your situation when your Norman uncle threatened your life. I suddenly had a vision of a sword hovering over your head about to strike then I saw you in a punt escaping from Maeldubesburg. The problem with our gift is that it does not respect time. Sometimes I see the future, sometimes the past and sometimes the present. I did not know when you were in danger, so I called to you in the hope that if you were alive and if you had inherited my gift then you might have been drawn to me. As for Father Dominic, that is much easier to explain. He was visiting Llandaff Abbey nearby and had stopped by to visit me, as he often did. Just at that time, I had the vision of your danger, so he borrowed a horse to ride back to Wickselm and your mother. He wanted to wait there in case you fled to her for help. We had agreed that if he found you, he would bring you here to the sacred Rowan tree of Morgannwg. I have been coming every day to be here for you. Now, please come with me so we can talk in more comfort."

Aelfgar still did not move.

"Father Dominic is dead!" he said, surprised at the anger in his voice.

"Who was he? Why did he risk his life trying to save me?"

"That is sad news. Father Dominic was a good man. A warrior like your father. They had been through many battles together. He became sick of killing and withdrew from the world to become a monk. His loyalty to your father was such that he chose to live close to your mother to provide her with some protection and he kept in touch with Sigewulf and Aemma to be sure you were being well cared for."

Ffraid the Seer turned and walked into the forest and this time Aelfgar followed cautiously. After a short while they reached a clearing and in front of them was a small, thatched building with a wisp of smoke rising from the chimney. Ffraid stopped outside the door and again put her hand on Aelfgar's arm.

"Inside is someone who will prove beyond all doubt that I am who I say I am and that you can trust me with your future." With that she pushed open the door and stood aside to let Aelfgar step inside. He placed his hand on his dagger as he was not at all sure what to expect. The room inside was very dark and coming from the bright light outside Aelfgar had difficulty in seeing anything to begin with. Gradually his eyes became accustomed to the gloom, and he could just make out someone, a woman, sitting on a stool next to the fire. Before he could say anything, the woman spoke.

"My boy, it is so good to see you. We have been worrying about you."

Aelfgar instantly recognised her voice.

"Aunt Aemma, is it you? Is it really you? I was so sure I would never see you again. I was certain that Uncle Ralf had had you killed." With that he rushed forward to hug his aunt and without realising it he began to cry. Aemma put her arms around him, and they stayed like that for quite a while. Time stood still for Aelfgar as, for the first time in years, he felt safe. Ffraid had entered the cottage and had busied herself in the corner. Now she approached with a wooden plate of food.

"Here Aelfgar, eat this and then we can talk." Aelfgar suddenly realised how hungry he was and started devouring the bread and cheese set before him. Ffraid brought him a mug. Aelfgar took a sip and then drank the contents in one go. As he sat eating, Aelfgar studied the two women. One he had known all his life and one he had never met before today. When his Aunt Aemma had disappeared shortly after Sigewulf's murder, Aelfgar had felt so alone and isolated for it was his aunt he had always turned to for comfort and reassurance. She had been the buttress supporting him through his childhood, more so than his father, more than his mother and even more than his Uncle Sigewulf. He had been convinced that she had been murdered on his Uncle Ralf's orders and now she sat there in front of him. His aunt looked well, though a little older than he remembered. Finishing the last of the bread and cheese, he moved closer to his aunt.

"Aunt Aemma, is this woman my grandmother, as she says she is?" His aunt looked at his serious face. She was struck by the changes she could see in him. He was turning into a very handsome young man. She smiled to herself as she replied.

"Yes, my dear, she is". Aelfgar frowned.

"Then how is it that I never knew she existed, that no-one including you have never ever mentioned her?" His Aunt took both his hands in hers and looked him straight in the eye.

"Do you want the truth?" He gave her an irritated look.

"Yes, of course I want the truth". She let go of his hands and leant back in her chair.

"Well, the reason no-one mentioned your grandmother Ffraid is because your father forbade us to speak about her. He banished her for life from his and your presence."

"Why? Why would he banish his own mother? What had she done?"

Ffraid spoke before Aemma could reply.

"Let me answer that. Your father was an extremely determined man. He was single-minded even when he was your age. He had in his childhood been impressed with the tales of Anglo-Saxon heroes and had set his mind to become one himself, which of course he did. Your father was a good man but would stand for no-one contradicting his will. As his success and fame as a warrior grew, he set his eyes on becoming a Kings Thegn. Whilst his father, Angar Leofricson, was from a long line of Anglo-Saxon warriors, he had made a mistake that in Aethelwulf's eyes threatened his own ambitions. He had married me or, more to the point, had not married me. Unlike Angar and Aethelwulf, I am not a Christian. I come from a long line of Celtic ancestors all of whom believe in old magic. I had refused a Christian marriage and had insisted that our union ceremony was performed by the Druids. Angar was willing to accept this because he was very much in love with me. After Angar died, Aethelwulf became head of the household and he began to feel that my Celtic heritage undermined his claim to be an Anglo-Saxon hero and harmed his prospects of becoming a King's Thegn, particularly as the King was a devout Christian. So, your father ordered me to renounce my Celtic beliefs and to become a Christian and obtain a church blessing of my marriage to Angar. I refused and so Aethelwulf banished me." Aelfgar looked closely at Ffraid and could see that telling him about her banishment had taken its toll.

"But why did my father not want me to know about you?" Now she let out a deep sigh.

"Because he felt that I might taint your upbringing with my Celtic beliefs. His view of the world left no room for mystery and magic. As far as your father was concerned, such thoughts would undermine your education, which was to be based on the solid Anglo-Saxon foundations of honour, self-control, and control over those around you." Aelfgar turned to his Aunt Aemma.

"Is this true?" She looked back at him with a sad look on her face.

"Yes, it was exactly as Ffraid has said. Your uncle Sigewulf and I were tempted to tell you, but we did not wish to go against

Aethelwulf's orders. We have, however, secretly stayed in touch with Ffraid over the years. After all she was Sigewulf's mother as well as Aethelwulf's and she was your grandmother and had a natural interest in your life and well-being. This seemed to work well for a long time. Your father would be away fulfilling the duties he had worked hard for. Your mother was not interested in your day-to-day upbringing, so Sigewulf and I were able to comply with Aethelwulf's instructions on your education but still share your progress with Ffraid. This all changed of course when Ralf de Beauville arrived and murdered Sigewulf and abducted you. He made it impossible for us to stay in contact and I knew it was just a matter of time before he would have me murdered as he needed to break your ties with your Anglo-Saxon heritage. So, I came here to live with Ffraid."

Aelfgar went quiet as he studied his newly discovered grandmother. So, he thought, this little lady is the mother of my father and Uncle Sigewulf. He could not see any physical resemblance but something about her was familiar, maybe her calmness. He thought about his dream and her calling to him. He thought about her waiting for him under the Rowan tree and the quiet gentle way she had spoken to him. Yes, the more he thought about it the more he accepted that she was indeed his grandmother but, even so, he felt quite disconnected from her. Not surprising, really, considering that just a few hours ago he had not known that she existed. Aelfgar spoke.

"It is a pleasure to meet you Grandma. I am not sure what to call you." Ffraid smiled at him as did Aunt Aemma.

"Grandma will do. Yes, that will do nicely." Aelfgar now thought about what Aunt Aemma and his grandmother had said about his father. He looked at them both and tried to find the right words to use.

"What you said about my father seems wrong. I do not recognise him as the man you describe. To me he was always generous and only ever wanted me to be happy. Not at all selfish or unkind.

Ffraid spoke again.

"Please don't misunderstand us. Your father was a good man, but his view of the world was completely coloured by his ambition. That ambition was to make the world a better place for everyone. However, it was important to him that he should be viewed as a hero for doing so. Also, he insisted that it should be achieved his way and no other. He wanted you to grow up to take over the legacy of his good work. So, he did what he could to make you want to be just like him. He deliberately made you feel special and see him as your inspiration. He also removed any other influences, such as me, who may have caused you to see the world differently to him. He was a man of clear and definite purpose. He was strong willed, determined and driven but he was not evil like your Uncle Ralph. His intentions were the best. He did not mean to hurt or harm me. As far as he was concerned, it was simply a necessary consequence of his mission to create a better world for everyone."

Aelfgar was not sure he fully understood what he had been told but he had other questions that he wanted answering.

"Ralf de Beauville told me that my father was dead. He had heard it from another Norman who had recently arrived from Sicily. He told Ralf that my father had died in a battle on the island of Sicily. At first, I refused to believe it, but I have reluctantly accepted it because I knew that, if my father was still alive, then he would have come back home and killed Ralf and rescued me. But on our journey Father Dominic said something before he died that made me think that my father is still alive. Do either of you know if my father is still alive?"

Ffraid and Aemma exchanged glances to see who was going to answer Aelfgar's question. Aunt Aemma spoke.

"The truth is that we don't know. Like you, we concluded that the only thing that would keep Aethelwulf from returning to Maeldubesburg would be death, but Father Dominic raised doubts in our mind too. Father Dominic used to be a soldier and was with your father at the battle that Ralf mentioned. He saw your father in the distance fighting on foot and surrounded by many of their enemy. He himself was having a difficult time fighting off another group of foreign soldiers. He managed to escape to some nearby hills and in the morning returned to the battlefield in search of your father. There was no sign of your father's body but his shield had been left standing with its point rammed into the ground. Father Dominic believed that somehow your father has survived; either he had been captured or had escaped. Also, recently Father Dominic was on a visit to Escanceaster Cathedral when he bumped into a monk who he recognised as a fellow ex-soldier. This monk mentioned that he thought he had seen Aethelwulf, or someone who looked like him, in southern Sicily long after the battle. Father Dominic liked to think that Aethelwulf was still alive and would one day return. That is the primary reason he kept an eye on your mother and you and kept in touch with us."

Aelfgar became lost in thought. He suddenly turned to his grandmother and asked,

"Surely with your gift you must know if he is still alive?"

To which Ffraid replied

"Unfortunately, I don't. I have not been able to see anything about Aethelwulf, from the moment that he banished me." Aelfgar felt himself getting angry again, just as he had earlier in the day. None of this new information he was receiving was helping him in any way. Instead of getting clearer, things were getting more confusing. Turning to Ffraid, he could not help his frustration and anger spilling over into his words when he spoke.

"You told me, earlier that I have a gift like yours. Then you tell me your gift doesn't work. What is this gift and where does it come from and what use is it, if it does not work when it is needed?" Ffraid closed her eyes, concentrating on finding the right words to say.

"Aelfgar, believe me, if I could give you an explanation I would but I cannot. So much about our world and how it works is a mystery and defies explanation. Try as we may we do not understand the forces that affect our lives. The best we can do is to try to find a way to live with them and ideally find a way to use them to our advantage. When I was a little girl, I could not understand why and how I could see across time and space. I still do not understand but I have learnt to accept it as a gift and make use of it if I can, such as reaching out to you to help guide your way."

Aelfgar paused while he thought for a moment. Then he seemed to come to a decision and said,

"I had dream. In it I was standing in a battlefield surrounded by the bodies of dead soldiers in strange dress and in front of me was a shield standing upright in the ground. When I looked at the front of it there was my father's emblem. It was just as you said Father Dominic had told you. Does this mean anything?"

Aunt Aemma spoke first.

"Maybe you had picked this up from your conversations with Father Dominic?"

"No. I had the dream before I met Father Dominic."

Ffraid took Aelfgar's hand.

"Aelfgar, no-one can say what this means except you. Like me you are blessed with a gift; like me you will have to find your way of using it. When did you first notice that you had this insight? Aelfgar gave a laugh that sounded more like a snort.

"It has never happened before. The dream of you calling me and the dream of my father's shield are the first time anything like this has happened. Grandma, how do I make it happen again? I want to learn to use it. Will you help me?"

Ffraid let go of his hand.

"Well, my boy, first you must fully accept that you have this gift and tell yourself that you will be open to it whenever it wants to appear. That should help you be receptive to its messages. To initiate its use, you must learn to create a frame of mind that encourages it to appear. Once you have that, you need to direct it by asking it a question. The next bit is the hardest. You must be relaxed and patient. It may be a while before anything happens and then in a flash you will get your answer. If you get impatient and try to force it, then nothing will come back to you. Try it now. Calm your mind and slow your breathing down to the bare minimum.

Aelfgar closed his eyes and tried to do as his grandmother instructed. It was hard. As soon as he cleared his mind of one thought, another popped up to replace it. He knew that he was struggling and was about to give up when he became aware of a sound nearby; he realised that it was Aunt Aemma humming, just as she did when comforting him as a small child. As he concentrated on this familiar sound, his mind emptied except for the question "Is my father dead?" Suddenly there was a flash and he saw the rooftops of a strange city. There were many flat roofs with gardens on them. Also, all over the city, there were strange, pointed towers with men calling from them. The sun was very bright. Before him was a pool of fresh water that was fed by a fountain. He leant forward, towards the water and saw a reflection but it was not his reflection. Aelfgar saw his father, looking older and tired. Aelfgar had the overwhelming sense that his father was thinking about him and wanted to see him. Even more surprising was that as he lifted his head he spotted a painted wall across the courtyard. On it was a picture of a tree that was the same design as on the brooch that he had been given by Father Dominic. Before Aelfgar had time to think about it there was another flash, and he was back in the room with Ffraid and Aunt Aemma.

Ffraid was anxious.

"Well?"

"I believe my father is still alive. I had a vision of him in a foreign land looking older and worn. I could feel he was thinking of me."

Ffraid was now excited. "Did you recognise anything else in your vision?"

Aelfgar nodded "Yes, in my vision I saw a painting of a tree."

Aelfgar described the painting to his aunt and grandmother. He decided not to mention the brooch that Father Dominic had given him. He was not sure why, perhaps he was practising the secrecy that Father Dominic had emphasised.

"Do you know what this painting means?" he asked.

Ffraid had been looking off into the distance and returned her focus back to Aelfgar and answered his question.

"It is the Tree of Life. An old belief found in many lands and cultures. There is a version in the Celtic tradition. The Vikings have one too, as do many cultures in the Middle Eastern world and beyond. They vary a little from each other, but this is the central meaning. It is called the Tree of Life because it symbolises the cycle of life that all living things on earth must follow. The leaves on the trees symbolise every living thing in the world. The tree, its roots, trunk, and branches symbolise the fact that all living things are connected and are part of the same single life force. The various stages of the leaf development represent the stages of life from birth to death. The leaves on the ground symbolise the decomposition of the body and soul back into the single pool of life force."

Aelfgar was quiet, deep in thought. Aemma and Ffraid waited.

"I do not know what the significance is of the tree in my dream, but I am sure that my father is alive somewhere. In my vision he was different to the father I remember. He was changed in some way. I feel he needs me and that I must go and find him."

The two women exchanged glances and Ffraid spoke.

"Aelfgar, you are now of age, a young man, and it is right that you set and follow your own path. Where will you start your search?

Aelfgar thought and replied,

"I will go to Escanceaster to try and find the monk who told Father Dominic about seeing my father in Sicily. I'll try to find out more".

"How will you get there?"

"I haven't thought about that yet."

Aemma leant forward and looked Aelfgar straight in the eye.

"Why not stay here for a few days while we work out how you can get to Escanceaster and find this monk. Ffraid has some contact with the monks in Llandaff and she may be able to use their knowledge to find a way."

Aelfgar nodded, it would be nice to rest and to draw breath. In a period of two days his world had changed dramatically. He welcomed the chance to take stock and make sense of his new freedom. Ffraid showed him to a bed in the corner and he climbed onto it and immediately felt extremely tired. He was just about to fall asleep when a thought crept into his head.

"Do you think Ralf de Beauville is still hunting for me?" he said out loud. For the second time the two women exchanged glances. This time Aemma spoke.

"Of course, he will be furious that you got away from him, but he does not know where to start looking. Put him out of your mind for now. You are safe here. Now, try and get some sleep."

Aelfgar grunted his reply and was immediately asleep.

When he awoke Aelfgar could not remember where he was. He was aware of sunlight streaming through a small window above his head and he could hear laughter coming through with the sunlight. There were two voices; one was his aunt but the other, also feminine sounded younger. Again, there was a loud peal of laughter and Aelfgar went to see what was causing it. Opening the door, he could see his aunt at the well with a young girl possibly the same age as Aelfgar. They were peering down the well and laughing uncontrollably. Aelfgar went closer. The girl, who had bright red hair turned towards him and looked directly into Aelfgar's eyes. He stopped in his tracks. It was as if he had been dealt a blow to the head during weapons training. All he was aware of was a pair of green sparkling eyes still moist with tears of laughter.

"Ahh! Aelfgar, I was wondering when you would emerge from your bed" said his aunt, still chuckling at what he did not know.

"Here is your chance to be a hero. Rhiannon here has dropped her cloak down the well. Perhaps you would climb down and recover it." At this Aemma and Rhiannon burst out in to fits of laughter again. Aelfgar could not make out whether he was being set up to be made a fool of or whether they were laughing at an earlier incident. He approached the well and looked down and as he did two buckets of water were poured over his head. He struggled to catch his breath as he stood there with water dripping from every part of him. The peals of laughter that had accompanied his drenching subsided as the guilty pair waited to see how he reacted. He wiped his hair from his eyes and attempted to lean nonchalantly against the wall of the well. He succeeded initially but then his arm slipped, and he lost his balance and slid down the wall to end up sitting in the muddy pool of water at the base. The peals of laughter this time were by far the loudest mainly because they were added to by Aelfgar himself. Aelfgar had the sudden realisation that this was the first time he had laughed uncontrollably for years, in fact since before the arrival of his Uncle Ralf. He also had the weird feeling that he was on the verge of an adventure that was going to completely change his life. Aelfgar climbed to his feet smiling and was about to go indoors to dry himself by the fire when his aunt said "Aelfgar Aethelwulfson this is Rhiannon of Dinas Powys."

"Pleased to meet you." was his reply. He was again transfixed by those sparkling green eyes.

"Likewise." replied Rhiannon with a little smile.

Later, after Aelfgar had dried his clothing, Aemma explained that Rhiannon, who had now left, was the daughter of Llewellyn ap

Dafydd the local Chieftain. They were Ffraid's nearest neighbour and Rhiannon visited Ffraid and her often. For some reason, this news pleased Aelfgar.

Aemma also explained that Ffraid had gone to Llandaff to seek out her contacts at the Cathedral and would be back by sunset. Aelfgar sat outside in the sunshine and thought about the events that had led to him being there. He wondered what his uncle was doing about finding him.

Odo sat looking across the Severn to the far shore. He was angry, extremely angry. His life had been turned upside down thanks to that little Saxon runt. Having sailed with Ralf de Beauville as his sergeant-at-arms to invade England and having helped him take and hold the town of Maeldubesburg from the Saxons, he was now a penniless wanderer searching for revenge. Odo had to admit to himself that he was lucky to be alive as Ralf de Beauville had a ferocious temper and was extremely upset that the boy had run away. Odo had thought of running away himself instead of going to tell Ralf of his failure to keep the boy under guard but that was not Odo's way. He also thought about killing Ralf before he could strike Odo but again this was not his way. So, he did his duty and reported the boy's escape in person. When Ralf heard the news, he stormed out of the great hall to send troops to find the boy, cursing his nephew as he went. He returned to the hall later and summoned Odo.

"Odo, my first instinct was to kill you for your failure to obey my orders. Indeed, it would be no more than you deserve. However, on reflection I have decided to strip you of everything that you own and to expel you from my service and my territory. You must never return, or I will kill you if you do. Unless of course, you come back with my nephew, dead or alive. I do not care which, and then you will be reinstated to your position of sergeant-at-arms and in addition I will double your pay from that moment on. Now hand in your uniform and arms. You may keep your dagger and your horse. I want you gone by dawn."

Odo was about to leave the town through the Westport when one of the men who had previously been under Odo's charge returned from searching for the boy. The soldier's mouth was a mass of torn flesh and congealed blood which made it difficult for Odo to hear what he was telling the guard. The soldier had another horse in tow and over it was a body of another soldier. The guard took both the horses and the body and sent the soldier straight to Ralf de Beauville. Odo strolled over to the guard. It was Robert, one of Odo's gaming companions.

Robert spoke.

"Odo, I am sorry for your bad luck, and I hope you find the little shit. That was William and this was Thomas; the boy killed him. William says that the boy was helped by a monk, and he thinks the monk might be wounded. They had a boat and set off down the Severn towards the sea. "

Odo nodded his thanks, returned to his horse, and left.

That is how he ended up at the monastery in Llandaff. He had heard further up the river that the body of a monk had been found dead in a boat near Llandaff. He also found out that the monk was not from Llandaff but from Wickselm. No-one had seen an Anglo-Saxon boy, but Odo felt sure that he must be somewhere near-by. So Odo was sitting at spot where the boat and the body had been found and he was trying to decide what to do next.

As he sat there, a small cargo boat came into view as it sailed out into the estuary from the river. On the boat he could see a party of monks sitting looking straight ahead across the Severn towards Somerset. Just before the boat pulled out of sight, one of the monks turned back towards the shore and pulled back his hood. Odo leapt to his feet and ran towards the water to get closer for a better look. He could not make out the monk's features, but he was young and had long blond hair just like Aelfgar and not the usual monk's tonsure. Odo ran to his horse and headed for the harbour.

Aelfgar turned and stared ahead. He felt sad to be leaving Ffraid and Aemma and if he were to admit it, sad to be leaving Rhiannon. She was the reason he had turned to look back. She had said that she would ride to the hilltop to see him go. He had not been able to see her, but he was certain she was there. Looking back, he had realised that he was close to where he had left the boat with Father Dominic's body on board. Despite Father Dominic's instructions and his oath, he could not bring himself to tip Father Dominic's body into the river. He was glad, when Ffraid had returned from Llandaff, to hear that Father Dominic had been found and later buried at the monastery. Ffraid had also brought news that a party of monks from Llandaff were about to journey from Llandaff to the Abbey at Escanceaster to deliver some relics of St David. Ffraid had persuaded the Abbot to allow Aelfgar to accompany them disguised as a monk. So it was that Aelfgar sat on the cargo boat as it approached the harbour at Watchet.

Rhiannon had been on the hilltop to see Aelfgar sail away. She had held her horse back under the canopy of trees that lined the hillside. She had been pleased to see Aelfgar turn to look for her and would have ridden forward to wave to him had she not seen the warrior-like man leap to his feet and rush towards Aelfgar's boat before mounting his horse and riding towards Llandaff. Rhiannon wondered what that was all about and decided to follow the man at a distance.

When Rhiannon rode onto the harbour-side at Llandaff she saw the warrior-like man speaking to the ferryman. There was obviously a disagreement between them as their voices grew louder and louder and they began waving their arms about. The warrior-like man turned and mounted his horse, shouting at the ferryman as he went. Rhiannon waited a moment and then walked over to the ferryman.

"Hallo Huwyl, who's your friend?"

"Oh, hallo Rhiannon, he is no friend of mine, the bloody arrogant Norman. He wanted to know where the monks were going and then he wanted me to ferry him and his horse across to Watchett, but he had no money to pay me. His accent was so bad I could hardly understand him. He got angry when I refused and started shouting at me in French, so I started shouting at him in Welsh."

"Where has he gone now?"

"He has no choice but to ride back up the river to Gleawanceaster to cross at the first ford and then ride back down the far shore to Somerset."

"How long will that take him?"

"Probably two days or so"

"Huwyl, I am just going to find my brothers and then I will be back. Would you then take us across the river to Watchet and, before you ask, I do have the money to pay you?"

If Odo was angry before he was now ready to explode. He was furious that the ferryman refused to take him across the river but what made him even angrier was the fact he found himself without the money or authority to demand to be taken across. This loss of power was the fault of the boy and made Odo even more determined to kill him. Odo had thought about killing the ferryman and stealing his boat, but he knew that the river was full of tides and rocks and needed an expert navigator, which he was not. He had also thought about forcing the ferryman to take him across at knifepoint, but he could tell that the ferryman would resist, and he would end up having to kill him. So he had accepted that he had to ride the long way around and hope he could pick up the monks' trail when he got to Watchett. As he rode through the forest, it occurred to Odo that he was not used to making decisions about what to do next. He had spent most of his time being told what to do, firstly by his father and then by Lord Ralf. All his life he had felt lost and unsure without clear and definite orders. When he was a boy, he had helped his father in the stables and had grown to be bigger and stronger than the other boys in Beauville. His father was not a kindly man, probably because he had lost an arm in a fight when he was younger. He made up for his loss by having a strong opinion on everything. He never physically harmed Odo, but he used his authority as a parent to dominate Odo's will. Odo could not say whether his compliance to authority was created by his father or whether it was his inherent nature. In fact, Odo would never have thought about such things at all.

As he rode, Odo recalled the day he met Lord Ralf. Both were still boys. Ralf had been out riding with his friends and his favourite horse had gone lame. Luckily, Odo's father's stables were close by and so Ralf had left the group and led his horse on foot to the stables. Odo was working inside when he heard laughing coming from outside. When he went to investigate, he saw a gang of local boys standing in the way of young lord Ralf and his horse. They were jeering and making fun of this fancy youth brought down to earth by his horse's misfortune. Odo recognised instantly that this youth was someone important and pushed his way through the crowd of boys to stand in front of the young Ralf.

"Ignore them sir, they are just ignorant peasants. How can I help you?"

Ralf stood in front of Odo, clearly furious at the way he had been treated. Though he and Odo were of a similar age there were two main differences. Firstly, Odo was far bigger and muscular than Ralf and secondly, Ralf had a fire burning behind his eyes that gave him a look of someone much older.

"What is your name?" Ralf demanded.

"Odo, sir"

"My horse is lame, and I would like you to look at him and see what can be done. Before you do however, I would like you to do something else for me."

"Yes, sir and what would that be sir?"

"Choose one of these boys that have been laughing at me and beat him to within an inch of his life".

Odo did not hesitate. He turned, grabbed the nearest boy, who happened to be his best friend Guy, and punched him as hard as he could in the face. Guy reeled backwards into the other boys, who scattered to edges of the yard. Before he could recover, Guy was met by a kick at full force in the groin. He screamed as sank to his knees. Odo stepped forward and kicked Guy on the side of the head. Guy fell unconscious to the floor. Odo rolled him onto his back, put his foot on Guy's chest and looked directly at Ralf for his next orders. In that moment, some kind connection was established between them. Ralf could see that this Odo might be a useful person to have around, and Odo was drawn to Ralf's natural authority. Ralf decided to set Odo a test. Ralf pulled a dagger from his belt and held it out to Odo.

"Odo, take this knife and finish the bastard off."

Again, without hesitation, Odo took the knife and returned to the unconscious boy and slid the knife up under Guy's sternum and into his heart. Guy died with a small sigh.

Odo took the knife and wiped it clean using Guy's smock. When he had returned it to Ralf he said.

"Now sir, let me take a look at your horse."

The rest of the boys stood around in a state of shock but not for long because Ralf's friends suddenly rode up to the stables to see where he had got to.

Ralf explained what had happened and all the party, one by one, found themselves wanting to see this stable boy who acted so ruthlessly on Ralf's behalf.

Odo returned and waited for Ralf's signal to speak.

"Sir, your horse has a badly bruised fetlock and needs to be rested for a while".

"Thank you. Odo, do you have a horse that I may ride home on if I leave my horse with you until he heals."

"Yes sir, though our horse is not of the quality of your horse."

"Mmmh! Roland, come here!" shouted Ralf.

With that one of his companions rushed over.

"Yes, Lord Ralf."

"Give me your horse and take this boy's horse instead for the ride home."

"Yes, Lord Ralf."

Ralf turned back to Odo.

"Odo, do you live here by yourself?"

"No sir, this is my father's stable, and I live with him."

"Well, in a few days when my horse is healed enough to make the journey, bring it to me at the Castle in Beauville and tell your father that you will not be returning."

"Yes, Lord Ralf".

Odo wondered how many times since then he had uttered those words. Certainly, it was more than he could count.

Meanwhile, Rhiannon looked across at her two brothers. They were much older than her and certainly a lot bigger, but she was born to lead and they were born to follow. They were both great warriors and had killed many men in battle. They each recognised that Rhiannon was like their father. The men did not resent her for her natural easy-going authority, in fact they adored her for it. They had got used to her giving them instructions; she had been doing it since she could speak. The brothers would give their lives to save their sister. Rhiannon, for her part, loved her brothers and always tried to take care of them in her own way. From an early age Rhiannon had an instinct for what was going to happen before it happened. Sometimes she had a clear premonition and other times just a vague feeling. It was the latter feeling that she had experienced when she had seen the warrior-like man jump on his horse having seen Aelfgar sail by on the boat. She had felt a worry about Aelfgar's safety and having spoken to Huwyl, her concern had increased. She had decided that she should go after Aelfgar and warn him. She had thought a lot about Aelfgar. She could tell immediately on meeting him that he was someone special. He was not like any of the boys that she had grown up with. She could sense that he was meant to achieve great things. He did not attempt to mask his vulnerability with bluff and false bravado, and she could sense his generosity of spirit. He was by nature a person who was more comfortable giving than taking. Rhiannon and her brothers had brought their horses on the ferry with them, so she was hopeful of catching up with Aelfgar before the warrior-like man.

Aelfgar sat down amongst the band of monks as they rested at the end of the day. They were gathered around the market cross in the small town called Twyfordton. They were sitting in silence after sharing a meagre meal of hard bread and even harder cheese. One of the brothers walked from monk to monk with a large jug of water and filled each monk's cup. He, like all the other monks, treated Aelfgar as if he was one of them. They had made good progress since they had landed at Watchet the previous afternoon. The monks had set a steady but relentless pace and reckoned to be in Escanceaster by evensong tomorrow. The group were just about to move on to St Peter's Church, on the other side of the river where they planned to stay the night, when the sound of galloping horses caught their attention. Aelfgar, like the rest of the group turned to see a young red-headed girl accompanied by two burly men ride towards them at full speed. At first Aelfgar did not recognise Rhiannon, then on doing so he ran towards her. With great dexterity she pulled on the reins so that her horse came to a halt in front of Aelfgar and in one continuous movement she leapt from horse and threw herself into his arms. Aelfgar was taken by surprise and almost lost his balance. Rhiannon stepped back and looked at Aelfgar with those amazing green eyes.

"Thank the Gods you are safe. I was afraid that the warrior had got here before me."

Aelfgar was struggling to understand what was happening and by the way they were all staring at Rhiannon and him, so were his companions.

"I am sorry, Rhiannon, but I do not understand what you are talking about."

Rhiannon told him about how she had come as promised to wave goodbye, had seen the warrior-like man and then about her conversation with Huwyl the ferryman.

Aelfgar felt sure that the man must be Odo sent by his uncle to recapture him or worse. Rhiannon introduced Aelfgar to her brothers, Tomos and Arwyn. Tomos felt that if Odo had kept going and had not stopped to eat or sleep then he could be closing in on Aelfgar at that very moment. Aelfgar had little time to decide what to do. After a short discussion with the senior monk, the group moved on to St. Peter's church as planned.

Odo entered Twyfordton an hour later and after asking anyone he came across whether they had seen a party of monks, he made his way to St Peter's church. As he approached, he could see light shining through the church windows and he could hear evensong being sung inside the church. He stood outside trying to decide what to do next. He was close to catching the boy and taking him back to Lord Ralf and regaining his old place in Ralf's service. Odo thought "What would Lord Ralf order me to do if he were here right now." The answer was easy. He would tell Odo to storm into the church, kill anyone who tried to stop him, kill the boy, drag his body out, throw it over his horse and ride back to Maeldubesburg. So that is what Odo did. As soon as he crashed through the door, the monks stopped singing and stared at him. No-one moved except Odo. He rushed towards the nearest monk grasping his dagger ready to strike at anyone who moved. He swept the monks hood from his head. It was not Aelfgar. Odo continued, monk after monk, until there was only one monk left. As Odo approached, the monk slowly raised his hands and removed his own hood. It was not Aelfgar. Odo screamed at the monks

"Where is he? Where is that little bastard?" The senior monk stepped forward.

"If you are referring to the Saxon boy who was travelling with us, he is not here. He left us earlier with some friends. He was going to travel back to Wickselm to seek his mother's help." Odo stood there, looking at the Monks who were all looking back at him. What now? He turned and strode out of the church. He had not reached his horse before the monks resumed their singing. As he rode off, the monk who was last in line and had removed his own hood stepped out of the church and smiled. Arwyn watched and hoped that Odo was on his way to Wickselm and not heading towards Escanceaster where his sister, brother and the Saxon lad were already heading.

As they rode, Rhiannon and Aelfgar talked.

"Rhiannon, I am grateful to you and your brothers for chasing after me to warn me about Odo. You have almost certainly saved my life. Your intuition was well founded. It feels a bit strange, after the last four years of living with my uncle, to have someone go out of their way to look after me." Rhiannon laughed. "Don't be silly! I would have done it for anyone. You would have done it for me. Anyway, I believe that if you are given the opportunity to help someone you should grab it with both hands."

"Don't get me wrong. It is just that I am not used to the idea of doing someone else a kindness for no reward."

"It is one thing to offer aid to someone for some reward but what really matters is taking the opportunity to help someone when there is no reward; that is even more reason for doing it. Anyway, I do get something out of it. I get the personal satisfaction that comes from doing the right thing. I also believe that if you give freely without expecting anything in return then someone will someday do something for you. After all, we are all part of the world in which we live."

Aelfgar rode alongside Rhiannon for a while quietly thinking about what she had said.

"I don't know why but what you just said feels right to me. Not like the things that Uncle Ralf has been telling me. He believes in the complete opposite. He believes that no-one cares for you, so you must help yourself by whatever means necessary. I have never been able to accept that as a way for me to live."

"He sounds very foolish. I believe the same law of the universe that rewards a generous act with a future generous act also repays acts of self-interest and aggression with return acts of a similar nature upon the person who commits them."

Aelfgar looked back to the time when Father Dominic died saving him from the Norman soldiers. He would always be grateful for his sacrifice. Suddenly he thought about the emblem on the brooch given to him by Father Dominic.

"Rhiannon, what do you know about the Tree of Life? Ffraid started to tell me about it, but we ran out of time."

Rhiannon turned and smiled at Aelfgar.

"That is what I am talking about. I am a Celt like Ffraid, and I believe in the Tree of Life. I see myself as a small leaf of the Tree of Life. I believe that everybody in the world is also a leaf on the tree and we are all part of the same tree. I believe that we should care for all other leaves on the tree as we would care for ourselves. So, in a way my helping you is also helping me as we are all part of the same living thing. Furthermore, I also believe that we should help those who would harm us so that in the long run their bad behaviour is nullified by our good behaviour. I believe that when we eventually die our body, soul and life force decompose and are recycled to provide life, wisdom and energy for the next leaves that appear on the tree after us."

"But what about those people who are like my Uncle Ralf, does their negative energy and evil soul get recycled?"

"Yes, unless we have countered their evil so that they no longer do acts of harm to others."

"But it will take an eternity to wipe out all evil in the world."

"Yes, Aelfgar, that is the point. Even though we will not live to see the result we must never stop helping others, never stop giving rather than taking. Even if they do not deserve it."

They rode on in silence until they were close to Escanceaster. At the bottom of a steep hill, they stopped but before they could start speaking again Tomos came riding up from behind where he had been checking that Odo was not still on their trail.

"Rhiannon, the road behind is clear. There is no-one following us. We need to return to Twyfordton to pick up Arwyn and get back to Llandaff before Father sends an army out to look for us. Aelfgar, I am afraid that you will need to finish your journey to Escanceaster on foot as we need to take Arwyn's horse back with us."

Saying goodbye to Rhiannon was one of the hardest things that Aelfgar had ever done. As he watched them ride away, he felt empty and unsure of himself once more. Something about Rhiannon's self-confidence and positive nature had lifted Aelfgar's spirit but it turned out to be temporary. Turning towards Escanceaster, he allowed his thoughts to tumble about in his head as he walked. Why was he so set on finding his father? Was he just chasing a dream? What would he get by seeing his father again? Or was this quest just an excuse to run as far as he could from his uncle? Should he abandon his search before it was too late and follow Rhiannon back to Llandaff? Aelfgar reached the top of the hill and there below lay Escanceaster. It was very impressive, with its high stone walls surrounding the entire city. Aelfgar stood gazing at the city below him, and he realised that he had changed since leaving Maeldubesburg. Whereas before when thoughts tumbled around his head, he would feel confused and lost; he now felt calm and relaxed. He was quietly confident that things would sort themselves out in time. He did not have any answers yet but was sure they would come. Perhaps being with Rhiannon had changed him after all? He decided to continue to Escanceaster and try to find the monk who had told Father Dominic that his father was still alive. Once he had done that, whether successful or not, he would consider what to do next.

Aelfgar entered the city through the West Gate. The guards on the gate were more interested in a young girl carrying a basket of fish on her head than in him. He made his way to the centre of the city looking for the Abbey, which turned out to be attached to the Cathedral of St Pauls. However, when he found the Abbey, he realised that he had no idea of how to go about finding the monk he was seeking. For a while he wandered around the walls that enclosed the Abbey without coming up with any ideas, As he was feeling tired and hungry he decided to sit down on a bench that was set against the Cathedral wall. There he lost himself in thought but still could not think of any easy way to find the monk. Gradually coming out of his reverie, he noticed that opposite there was a row of houses and that one of them had an ornate carved door. As he studied the door, he realised that the carving was a stylised version of the Tree of Life. Was this just a coincidence or was this one of the signs that Father Dominic had told him about? Aelfgar reached deep into his pocket to retrieve the brooch and pinned it upside down on his cloak as instructed by Father Dominic. He then plucked up his courage to go over and knock on the door. There was no reply, so he knocked again, this time a bit harder. Still no reply, so Aelfgar turned the big iron door handle and stepped through. Instead of entering a house as he had expected, he found himself in a large courtyard. All around the courtyard there were shops and houses. On the opposite side of the courtyard to the door that he had just used was an archway which opened onto the city's main street. The courtyard was busy with people coming and going. Many of them were visiting an inn called the Red Dragon. Aelfgar decided to spend some of the money that Aunt Aemma had given him. He sat down at a table outside the inn and looked around. He was not sure what he was expecting to happen next. People were coming and going, and none seemed to pay him any attention. After a few minutes, he was served by large woman with plump arms. As she took Aelfgar's order, she noticed his brooch.

"Excuse me, luvvie, but you've put ya brooch on upside down."

Aelfgar thought

"This is clearly not someone from the secret society" so he said "'Have I? I am always doing that."

She chuckled and went off into the inn.

Shortly afterwards, the woman reappeared with Aelfgar's broth and beer. Just behind her followed a man carrying a mug. Aelfgar paid her and had started dipping the bread into the broth when the man who had followed the woman out sat down at Aelfgar's table and leant forward so that he was uncomfortably close to Aelfgar's face. He then started speaking in Latin.

"I am looking for the house of the Lord. Can you help me?"

Aelfgar replied as instructed.

"I am a stranger here myself. I am looking for a place to rest."

The man smiled as he said,

"There are places to rest in the house of the Lord."

Again, Aelfgar replied as instructed.

"Well, perhaps we can look together."

The man replied

"Yes, let's start by looking down this way."

Aelfgar reluctantly left his meal and followed the man.

They went through the archway and into the main street, which they crossed and disappeared down a narrow alley way which twisted and turned before opening into a small square. The man suddenly grabbed Aelfgar and pulled him into a doorway. Here they waited for what seemed a long time to Aelfgar. When it was clear, they crossed the square and entered a tiny church through a side door. The church was empty and in fact looked like it had not been used in a while. They went down the aisle and into an adjoining room. Unlike the church, this room looked like it had been used frequently. The man lit a candle and gestured to Aelfgar to take a seat at a table in the middle of the room. Aelfgar studied the man. He was old. He had a lot of white hair and sparkling blue eyes,

"Now, before we get down to business, I need you to tell me how you came to possess the brooch."

Aelfgar told the man who he was, about his flight from Maeldubesburg, how Father Dominic had saved him but had been mortally wounded and how he had given the brooch to Aelfgar and instructed him on how to use it.

"I am sorry to hear of Father Dominic's death. He was a good man. It does not surprise me that he died saving someone else's life. If you are to continue to wear Father Dominic's brooch you should know that you also carry with you a responsibility to live up to his example."

"I know very little about Father Dominic other than what I have just told you."

"Well, we will come back to that. As you will have deduced, Father Dominic and I are members of a secret society. It was set up centuries ago originally to help and protect pilgrims. Our mission has over the years expanded to give aid wherever and whenever it is needed and sought. You have come here seeking assistance so how may I help you."

Aelfgar told him about Father Dominic's dying words about his father and that he was in Escanceaster seeking the monk who had been a soldier alongside Father Dominic and Aethelwulf.

The man stood up and walked around the room deep in thought.

110

"Clearly you cannot return home to your uncle as your life would be in danger and I can see that as you think your father is alive, you must try to find him. I will make some inquiries and see if I can find this monk that you seek. It may take a few days. Are you happy to stay here until we get any news?" Aelfgar nodded. "

And one last thing; "Are you certain that you want to find your father?"

"I have been asking myself that same question recently. I had been told and had accepted that he was dead, having died fighting for his King. Then I met Father Dominic who made me think that he was still alive. Originally, I wanted to know if he was dead or alive and if he was alive, ask him why he had never returned to Maeldubesburg to rescue me from my uncle Ralf de Beauville. Then I had a vision and saw my father alive in a foreign place and I had the strong sense that he needed me. Now with what has happened since I started out searching for him, I feel that the journey to find him is as much about finding myself as well."

The man sat down again.

"I have heard of people who have visions and see things denied to the rest of us. Were there any clues in your vision as to where he could be?"

Aelfgar described the dream and told the man about the painting on the wall depicting the Tree of Life. The man was fascinated by this and asked questions about the style of the painting and the roof tops and towers that Aelfgar had seen.

"I must leave you now. Please stay here. I will return shortly with some food and drink for you."

"Thank you but I just realised I do not know who you are. I don't know what to call you."

"I know and it must stay that way. We never give our names in the society."

"I don't understand. Why is it necessary for the society to be so secret?"

"As I said earlier, our mission is to give help where help is needed and sought. We feel that if we do this publicly then there is the danger that we might be tempted to do this not solely for the benefit of the recipient but for the acclaim and good reputation our deeds generate. We believe it is best for the people we help and for ourselves that we remain anonymous."

"But how will I be able to repay you later if you are able to help me find my father?"

"By doing something good for someone else, without wanting anything in return. Now I must go."

After he had gone, Aelfgar sat quietly thinking about his earlier conversation with Rhiannon and the conversation he had had with the man who had just left. He thought about how strange it was that before leaving Maeldubesburg he had never heard of the Tree of Life or the meaning it seemed to have for some people. He reflected on how he had grown up looking to his father as a hero but at the same time never thinking that he ever wanted to become a hero like him. Also, he had known from the moment he first saw his Uncle Ralf that he could never be like him. Aelfgar tried to think who he was most like of those who had been around him as a child. He had little in common with his mother who seemed to live in a world of her own making and did not seem at all concerned about those around her. Aelfgar had admired his Uncle Sigewulf, who Aelfgar remembered with fondness. Uncle Sigewulf had always treated him fairly and with a gentle touch but there was never a real bond between them. Aelfgar thought about his Aunt Aemma and decided it was her he was most like. She was of a generous nature and seemed to get pleasure from helping those around her including Aelfgar. Aelfgar remembered that even though he had been good at his weapons training, he had never enjoyed it and had never liked the idea of killing people. He had been most happy when he was working among the villagers bringing in the harvest. Aelfgar thought back to the Norman soldier he had killed protecting Father Dominic. He had not hesitated in stabbing the soldier, but he had taken no pleasure from the act. Equally, he had not felt any guilt afterwards because if he had he not done so, the soldier would have killed Father Dominic. He had acted in defence and only as a last resort. Having this time to think was useful, thought Aelfgar. I have never considered myself in these terms before. His thoughts were suddenly interrupted by the man returning with the promised food and drink.

"I have started making enquiries about the monk that you are seeking. I hope to have some initial information in the morning. You must sleep here tonight, and I will return in the morning".

Aelfgar watched him leave before turning his attention to the plate of bread and meats in front of him. After eating his fill he found a corner to lie down and was soon asleep.

At this point in the book, Stevie realised that she needed to take a break. She looked up and saw that it was getting dark outside and switched a lamp on beside her. She had found it fascinating to learn more about the Tree of Life. There was something compelling about the philosophy and character of the Tree of Life organisation that appealed to her personal values. She felt that she was also beginning to understand what it was that Mrs Joan Spencer had been trying to convey and how it was more than a hostage rescue organisation. She quickly made herself a hot drink and returned to the book.

Chapter 6

Inner Depths

Aelfgar looked out at the sea and the dark clouds rushing towards him. Once more he was on a cargo boat crossing the water in pursuit of his father and his own fate. However, this time he was not a passenger but a crew member. The unnamed man had eventually returned with news about the individual that Aelfgar sought. The news was a mix of bad and good. The man had discovered that the monk had died over a year ago but fortunately he had found another member of the brotherhood who had been present when the original conversation about Aethelwulf had taken place. This monk also remembered that, after the conversation, his dead compatriot had recalled some more information about Aethelwulf but had not been able to tell Father Dominic as he had already left. This new information was that when the dead monk had seen the man who looked like Aethelwulf in Messina, the man was boarding a ship that was heading for Reggio Calabria. The white-haired man also told Aelfgar that he had spoken to some other members of the society and they were certain that the place that Aelfgar had seen in his vision was Cordoba. Aelfgar concluded that the choices before him were either to travel to Cordoba or give up his quest. Aelfgar's instincts had told him that if he gave up his search now, he would regret it for the rest of his life. Nearly two weeks passed before a way was found for Aelfgar to travel to Cordoba. Somehow or other the man was able to arrange a passage for Aethelwulf from Escanceaster to Cadiz, the nearest port to Cordoba. He explained that Aethelwulf would have to work for his passage as a member of the crew. Aelfgar protested that he knew nothing about sailing a boat. The man explained that this had been taken care of as the first part of the journey would be crossing the channel to Barfleur in Normandy. During this time the captain and crew would teach him all he needed to know. As it turned out, Aelfgar seemed to be a natural sailor. He only needed to be told something once and he managed to grasp the task straight away. The interplay of wind, sail, tides and steering all made sense to him and by the time the ship had reached Barfleur, he was accepted by the rest of the crew, Eadric and Hrodulf. The captain was a gruff Saxon who reminded Aelfgar of his Uncle Sigewulf. They were both direct in the way they spoke, not wasting time with unnecessary words but always fair and acknowledged good work if only by a grunt. During the stop at Barfleur, they loaded the ship with barrels of salted fish and took on board a passenger. He was an elderly man, dressed in a manner Aelfgar had never seen before. He wore a long tunic that was like a monk's habit together with a heavy cloak slung over his shoulders. He was clutching a large bag which was very heavy from the way that he carried it. He had a very pronounced stoop and his hair was shaved at the front and at the back, but the side hair was long and hung in ringlets. On the top of his head he wore a small circular cap. The most striking feature was his nose. Not only was it large but it had a magnificently hooked shape which, combined with his green eyes, gave him a hawk-like appearance. Despite his years the new passenger walked in a sprightly manner and moved about the boat with confident steps. The tide turned just before lunch and they set sail again following the coast westwards. The hawk-like passenger settled himself in the small tent at the stern of the boat and stared silently out to sea through the open flap. That evening they turned southwest making good speed with a strong northerly wind. The crossing of the Bay of Biscay passed very smoothly. Eadric and Hrodulf had told Aelfgar stories of crossings they had made previously that had filled him with dread. Luckily, he never got to experience the gale force winds and enormous waves that they had told him about. So it was that four days later they arrived in A Coruna in northern Spain.

As Aelfgar made ready to leap off the bow of the boat onto the quayside, he reflected on how happy he felt. Somehow being at sea and engrossed in his duties had led him to forget about his real life, his Uncle Ralf, Odo, Father Dominic, Aunt Aemma, Ffraid and even Rhiannon. He had not entirely forgotten about his father, but he did not think about him as he had done in the past, obsessed with whether he was alive or not. He now thought of his father as a destination; like a place to be sought and discovered. Aelfgar leapt with confidence, landing comfortably next to the mooring bollard and immediately secured the bow line while Eadric secured the stern line. Aelfgar looked up at the captain and when the captain turned his gaze in his direction, Aelfgar shouted "All secure Captain." Later, when he was helping to unload the cargo, he wondered why working on a boat seemed so natural to him. He felt very content making a worthwhile contribution to the work, just like at harvest back in Maeldubesburg.

As he was stacking the cargo that he had just helped unload, two Norman knights approached him and started speaking to him in Spanish. Their manner was brusque and impatient, which immediately annoyed Aelfgar. In response, he looked at them blankly and shrugged his shoulders and said in Saxon

"I do not understand you. Do you speak Saxon?"

The older of the two was clearly irritated and this time spoke in French.

"Listen, you imbecile! is this boat sailing to Cadiz?"

Aelfgar's chose to forget that he could speak French.

So again, he replied in Saxon

"I do not understand you. Do you speak Saxon?"

This time the elder Norman reached for his sword but the younger one grabbed his arm before he could grasp the handle.

"Let us not draw attention to ourselves. He is clearly an idiot. Let us find someone else to ask."

Just at that moment the captain came along. Speaking to Aelfgar, he said

"What's up, lad? Who are your friends?"

"I don't know Captain. I can't understand them."

The captain turned to the two Normans and, switching to Spanish, asked if he could be of help.

"Yes, we are seeking passage to Cadiz, and we were trying to find out from this moron if your boat is going there" said the older Norman still irritated.

"Well, it is and there is room on board for a couple more passengers if they are able to pay."

The Norman reached inside his tunic and brought out a large shiny gold coin.

"Will this cover the cost?" he said aggressively, knowing that the coin was worth a lot more than the cost of the journey.

The captain looked at the coin and then he looked at each of the Normans and asked,

"Do you have anything you need to bring with you?"

"No, we are travelling light. How long will it take to get to Cadiz?"

"You can never be certain, but I would say it will take at least three or four days. We sail on the evening tide so you should be there by Friday lunchtime."

"Fine, but we have to take care of some business before we leave but don't worry, we will back well before you sail."

As they strode away the captain turned to Aelfgar and asked him what he thought about the two Normans.

"They are typical Normans; unfriendly, only interested in getting what they want. There is something else about them that made me feel uneasy, but I am not sure what it was."

"Look, lad, I think your instincts are spot on. I would wager all my cargo that they are up to no good. I want you to keep an eye on them during the journey and let me know if there is anything for me to worry about. Do you think that you can do that?"

"Yes Captain, I will stay close to them."

That evening, after they had set sail, Aelfgar settled himself amidships close to where the two Normans were sitting together. They were talking quietly in French. They kept themselves separate from the crew and the other passenger, who for his part seemed to want to keep his distance as well.

During the night Aelfgar noticed that the two Normans never slept at the same time. One of them was always awake keeping watch. This is how the journey continued. The only time either of the Normans spoke to anyone other than each other was when Aelfgar took them their food at mealtimes and then it was only to curse him for being an idiot.

Four days later they were approaching land and could see the skyline of Cadiz clearly on the horizon. The hawk-like man, who up until this point had remained in his tent, went, and stood on the bow of the boat with his eyes fixed on the city as it grew larger and larger. The two Normans remained huddled together amidships but were equally transfixed by the looming city of Cadiz. As the boat approached the quayside Aelfgar noticed that there was a group of soldiers waiting for the ship to dock. Aelfgar approached the captain and when the captain was not preoccupied with steering the boat safely alongside the quay, he asked him about the soldiers.

"I don't know lad. I have made this journey many times and I have never been met like this before. Stay on board with the others while I go and find out what they want."

The captain turned to the rest of the crew and passengers and told them to stay on board whilst he went and spoke to the soldiers. The hawk-like man seemed very agitated and concerned and was pacing up and down. The Normans were standing close together looking fierce, with their hands resting on their swords. The captain was back a moment later and called Aelfgar to him.

"It seems they are looking for spies and agents from the Spanish northern territories. They are meeting every boat to find out where it sailed from and then they are searching everyone on board and questioning them. Aelfgar, position yourself close to the Normans and let me know immediately if there is anything you think I should know."

The captain then went and spoke to the hawk-like man, who seemed to get even more agitated and started to wring his hands. Aelfgar followed the captain over to the Normans and started coiling a rope quietly nearby. The Normans reaction to the news was completely different. They started swearing and striding over to the side of the boat and glaring menacingly at the soldiers. The Captain, Eadric and Hrodulf left the boat and went over to the soldiers who started searching their clothing and asking them questions. From a distance it looked friendly enough, though the soldiers seemed very thorough in their searches. The Normans suddenly stopped swearing and, seemingly unaware of Aelfgar, switched to speaking in Latin.

"We cannot let them search us like that. They will certainly find the letters that we are carrying from the Holy Father to the Bishop of Cordoba. It will be our death warrant if they do. We must destroy them before we get off the ship."

"But if we do that, we will have nothing to use to convince the bishop to help us."

"We could hide them on the ship and come back for them later when the fuss has died down."

"But what if they search the ship and find them?"

"Yes, that would be a problem. What if we hide one of the copies and let them find the other on someone else? Then they will probably not want to search any further."

"But who could we use, the captain and most of his crew are already being searched? There is just the old man and the imbecile boy."

"It will have to be the old man."

"You are right, go and slip your copy of the letter into his bag or pocket while I hide my copy behind those barrels over there. Be careful, we can't afford to get caught."

They turned and suddenly became aware of Aelfgar. The elder Norman once again made to draw his sword but again the younger one stopped him.

"Are you crazy, the last thing we need is for you to kill this boy in front of these soldiers. He could not hear us and even if he did, he would not have understood us speaking in Latin. Now let us get on with our plan before it is too late."

Aelfgar hurried off and went to stand where he had a clear view of the hawk-like man. The man was bent over. It looked like he was replacing a plank in the decking. He must have felt Aelfgar watching him because he suddenly stood up and stepped away from that spot. In doing so his cloak slipped from his shoulder and dropped on to the deck at the feet of the approaching Norman. Out of the corner of his eye, Aelfgar saw the hawk-like man retrieve his cloak and, in his agitation, struggle to drape it back over his shoulders. The Norman saw his chance and, stepping forward, he began to help the man rearrange his cloak. Aelfgar watched as the elder Norman slipped the parchment into the hawk-like man's cloak pocket. Instantly he knew what he had to do. He could not let an innocent man be captured, perhaps even killed, while the two Normans were left free to carry out their underhand activities. Once the elder Norman had returned to his comrade amidships, Aelfgar moved closer to the hawk-like man who was watching the soldiers finish searching the captain and the others. He could see the end of the parchment protruding from the cloak pocket. Just then, the captain called for the hawk-like man to come ashore and take his turn to be searched. The man turned and, not realising that Aelfgar was right next to him, stumbled into him. Aelfgar used this moment of confusion to extract the parchment from the pocket and stuff it inside his jacket. Now the Normans joined Aelfgar at the top of the gangplank and watched as the hawk-like man approached the group of soldiers. Aelfgar realised that the hawk-like man was not carrying his sack. He must have hidden it on the boat somewhere. Perhaps that was what he was doing a few moments ago. One of the soldiers removed the hawk-like man's cloak and searched it thoroughly, then threw it on to ground and started to search him from head to toe. The two Normans looked at each other puzzled that the soldiers had not found the parchment. But before they could speak, the captain called for them and Aelfgar to come ashore and be searched. Aelfgar let the Normans go first and waited until they had nearly reached the soldiers when he ran after them. They heard his footsteps and turned to see Aelfgar approaching. He seemed to lose his balance and fall heavily into the younger one. Both the Normans reacted by drawing their swords. Immediately the soldiers stepped forward, with their swords also drawn, and surrounded Aelfgar and the Normans. It became very tense with everyone poised to act but at the same time not wishing to provoke a fight. Aelfgar, who was on the floor in front of the younger Norman, looked across at the captain who took command of the situation.

"You stupid boy, come and stand over here while they search these two Knights."

At this the Normans sheathed their swords and relaxed a little as did the soldiers. The officer in charge indicated for the older

Norman to step over to be searched by two of his men. The other Norman was also being searched. The rest of the men stood watching ready to react if the Normans made any kind of move towards their swords again. In the second group, the young Norman was amazed when one of the soldiers searching him produced a parchment from under his cloak. The Norman went to grab the parchment and immediately he found himself with four or five swords at his throat. The officer took the parchment and began to read, and as he did his face became more and more tense. He suddenly barked an order and both Normans were grabbed and disarmed. The officer approached the captain. After a short conversation, he gathered his men and the two Normans, then marched off towards the city.

"I knew they were up to no good. You did well to keep watch on them, though you nearly got yourself killed at the end. What was that all about?"

Aelfgar decided not to tell the captain what he had done so he just said.

"I suddenly panicked when I realised that I was going to be the last one to be searched so I ran to catch up but lost my footing and fell into them accidentally."

"Well, back to work. I know you are leaving us here but not until we are unloaded. I will be sorry to lose you. You have been a good addition to the crew. Now, let us get back on board and start unloading."

As soon as he was back on board, Aelfgar made his way to look for the other parchment which had been hidden behind the barrels stored amidships. After a few moments he found it and quickly hid it within his blouse. He looked up to make sure no-one had seen him, but all attention was on the hawk-like man who was leaving the ship, this time clutching his bag. Aelfgar began unloading the barrels and sacks that made up the cargo. As he did this, he reflected on the incident with the two Normans. Aelfgar felt no remorse in causing their arrest. Though he did not know the reason they were coming to southern Spain nor what was written in the Pope's letters that they were carrying, he was certain he had averted some wrongdoing. He also thought about the hawk-like man and took quiet pleasure from the fact that he had prevented him from falling victim to the Norman's nasty plot. As he was rolling the last barrel across the quayside to stand it with the others by the wall the captain called to him.

"Aelfgar, come here lad. You are all done. It is time for you to head off now. Just one last thing; if you are heading into Cadiz perhaps you could offer to help our passenger as he seems to be struggling to carry that sack of his." pointing towards the hawk-like man in the distance. With that he shook Aelfgar's hand and turned to shout at Eadric and Hrodulf.

Aelfgar caught up with the hawk-like man at the beginning of the long and cobbled road that led up from the harbour into the town of Cadiz. The hawk-like man was resting by the side of road. Carrying his sack was clearly taking its toll on him. He looked up anxiously as Aelfgar approached. Aelfgar spoke to him in French.

"Excuse me, sir, but the captain sent me to offer to carry your sack into town for you."

The hawk-like man looked closely at Aelfgar.

"Ah! you can speak French. Well, well, I had you down as a simple Saxon. Anyway, your captain is very kind, and even though my pride wants me to turn down your offer, my common sense says thank you and yes please."

So Aelfgar took up the sack and was surprised by how heavy it was. The hawk-like man must be much stronger than he looked to have carried it this far. Aelfgar threw the sack over his shoulder and started towards the town. Without his burden the hawk-like man seemed to brighten and relax.

"What's your name boy? People call me Mordecai ben Levi."

"Sir, my name is Aelfgar Athelwulfson."

"A Saxon name. How come you speak French so well, Aelfgar?"

"My mother is Norman and insisted that I learn to speak French and Latin as well as Saxon."

Mordecai raised an eyebrow and switched to speaking in Latin.

"Aelfgar, there is a lot more to you than meets the eye. What are you doing working as crew member on a cargo ship?"

"I was working my passage to Cadiz. I had no money to pay the fare."

"Why did you want to come here to Cadiz?" Mordecai asked switching back to French.

"I am on my way to Cordoba to search for my father. I believe he is there and that he needs me."

"I am on my way to Cordoba myself to visit my brother. I am planning to organise transport when I get into Cadiz. Perhaps we could travel together?"

Aelfgar thought about this suggestion. It would certainly solve the problem of how to get to Cordoba. Perhaps also Mordecai's brother might be able to help him find his father or at least get him started looking in the right places; so he agreed. Mordecai seemed pleased at this.

As they approached the town, they heard bells ringing. Something about the urgent nature of the bells seemed to indicate that they were an alarm of some kind being sounded. As they got closer, they could see that the gate had been shut and there were guards on the road stopping people approaching and getting any closer to the town.

Mordecai and Aelfgar were forced to wait with a small crowd of merchants, sailors and townsfolk until the gates were re-opened an hour or so later and everyone was allowed to proceed. There was a murmuring coming from within the walls, as if everyone were talking quietly throughout the town. Mordecai headed straight for the stables and speaking in Spanish, asked if there

124

were any horses for sale. The stable master looked at Mordecai and Aelfgar and seemed unsure as to what to answer.

"Is there a problem?" asked Mordecai.

"Well, yes and no!" said the stable master.

"What do you mean?"

"Did you hear the alarm bells ringing loudly an hour or so ago?"

"Yes"

"That was because two Norman captives killed their guards and escaped; until they have been recaptured, I am not permitted to provide horses to anyone. You had best check into the inn across the road and wait. I will come and find you when the fuss is all over and then you can take the horses."

So that is what Mordecai and Aelfgar did. They decided not to take a room because they hoped that they would not need it. Instead, they sat at a table in the bar and shared a simple meal. After a while Mordecai looked at Aelfgar and seemed to make his mind up about something.

"Aelfgar, on the boat I had the feeling that you were watching those two Normans and I felt you remove something from my cloak before I left the boat. I then saw you plant that parchment on the Norman. Why don't tell me what is going on?"

Aelfgar now had a decision to make. Based on his earlier thoughts brought about by his conversations with Rhiannon and the Man in Escanceaster, Aelfgar would have preferred to keep the matter to himself, but he instinctively knew that Mordecai would not trust Aelfgar unless he heard the truth.

" I will answer you, but before I do, I have a question that I would like to ask you. When we were approaching Cadiz on the boat and you saw the soldiers waiting for us you started to become extremely nervous and agitated. Not only that; from the moment you appeared at the quayside in Barfleur you have been clutching your sack, never letting it out of your sight except when you went to be searched. The sack is extremely heavy and I can hazard a guess as to what is in it. Perhaps, you can tell me what is going on."

Mordecai smiled.

"As I said earlier, there is a lot more to you than meets the eye. It seems that we must decide whether to trust each other."

Aelfgar suddenly realised that for the first time in his life he felt confident and sure of himself. He liked the feeling. Suddenly, he decided.

"You are right, and my instincts tell me that you are someone that I can trust so I will answer your question."

Aelfgar gave Mordecai a detailed description of what had happened. Mordecai listened intently and when Aelfgar had finished Mordecai said, "

"Do you still have the second parchment on you?"

Aelfgar dug deep into his tunic and pulled out the parchment. Mordecai frowned as he read it.

"Aelfgar my boy, I am incredibly indebted to you for saving me from certain imprisonment and probably execution. If I had been found with this on me, I would have been unable to defend myself, especially in the light of what I am about to tell you in response to your question. I am carrying a large amount of gold coins. I am taking them to my brother in Cordoba as he needs them to fund some venture of his that he is setting up there."

Aelfgar smiled inwardly; his instincts had been right.

"Why did you not travel with some protection, a guard or two?"

"I felt it might draw attention to me if I did. I felt it was better to travel quietly alone and hopefully, unnoticed."

Before they could talk any further the stable master appeared in the doorway and called them over.

"I have just heard that the Normans have managed to get out of town. They were spotted down by the quayside searching a boat but managed to get away again. Anyway, I can let you have your horses now."

Aelfgar was surprised to find himself growing fonder of Mordecai with every step of their journey. There was something about Mordecai's easy-going manner that made Aelfgar feel that they were meant to be friends. Despite their age difference, Mordecai treated Aelfgar as an equal and for Aelfgar this generated a strong feeling of respect towards Mordecai. Aelfgar recalled the conversations that he had had with Rhiannon when they had been approaching Escanceaster and he felt that by preventing Mordecai from becoming the victim of the Norman's plot he had somehow carried out Rhiannon's wishes. The more that he thought about how he had responded to his instinctive feeling of right and wrong the more satisfied he felt about himself. He also reflected on how he had felt before he had told Mordecai of what had happened and recognised that the original secrecy of the knowledge had increased his feeling of self-esteem. He then remembered the white-haired man who had helped him in Escanceaster and that now he could better understand his explanation of why the society insisted on secrecy. The fact that Mordecai now knew that Aelfgar had helped him seemed to have introduced a small imbalance into the relationship. Mordecai clearly felt indebted to Aelfgar.

They had briefly stopped at Seville to rest the horses and enjoy a meal. Now they were travelling again, approaching Cordoba. They were riding silently, each lost in their own thoughts, when Aelfgar noticed a movement in the rocks ahead. He eased his horse forward until he had caught up with Mordecai.

"I think we have company ahead perhaps waiting for us and given what you are carrying in your sack, I think we should try and go around them." Mordecai had noticed nothing but trusted Aelfgar's young eyesight and agreed. When they were out of sight of the rocks ahead, they left the road and followed a dried riverbed into the trees that covered the hillside. Aelfgar led

Mordecai up the steep gradient until they had reached the top of the hill. Leaving his horse with Mordecai he scrambled onto some rocks to gain sight of the road below. He easily found the spot where he and Mordecai had left it and moving his eyes along from there, he found the rocks where he had seen the movement. To his shock he could see the two Normans from the boat poised to attack. They were clearly waiting for someone. Did they know it would be Mordecai and Aelfgar coming along next? If so, why were they going to attack them? Aelfgar then recalled the stable master saying they had been seen searching a boat in Cadiz harbour. They must have been looking for the copy of the Pope's letter that they had hidden. Of course, when they had not found it, they must have realised that Aelfgar had been listening after all and had stolen it. They must have found out somehow that Aelfgar and Mordecai were on their way to Cordoba and managed to get ahead of them. As he watched Aelfgar saw the younger Norman leave his hiding place to peer down the road. It must have been a movement like this that Aelfgar had spotted earlier.

On returning to Mordecai, Aelfgar told him of what he had seen and they decided to try to reach Cordoba by staying in the trees and by moving parallel to the road. That night they camped in the woods, without a fire. In the morning they re-joined the road on the edge of Cordoba. It was busy with people coming and going. They had studied the scene for a good hour looking for any sign of the two Normans and around mid-morning they entered the town. They went straight to the stables and sold their horses before setting out for Mordecai's brother's house. It was situated high in the town overlooking the surrounding countryside. As they approached the house Aelfgar wondered whether his father was in Cordoba after all and if he would be able to find him. Mordecai knocked loudly on the door which was eventually opened by a man who looked so like Mordecai he had to be his brother. The two embraced for a long time before Mordecai introduced Aelfgar to his brother.

"Aelfgar this is my brother Avhram ben Levi. Avhram this is my companion Aelfgar Athelwulfson." The two shook hands but Avhram seemed distracted.

"Did you say Aelfgar Athelwulfson?" Turning to Aelfgar Avhram asked

"Where are you from Aelfgar?"

Puzzled Aelfgar replied

"Maeldubesburg in Angland."

Mordecai looked at his brother "Is there something wrong?"

"No, but I think you and I are in the process of witnessing a miracle." Turning to Aelfgar, Avhram then said

"Aelfgar, please follow me. I have someone I want you to meet."

With that he turned and led the travellers into an inner room. The room was pure white with a low table in the centre surrounded by low chairs. Seated in a shady corner on one of these was a man who was reading a large book. The man looked up and stared at the visitors with the blank look of someone who moments before had been lost in the contents of their book.

Avhram spoke to the seated man

"My dearest friend, it gives the greatest pleasure to introduce you, not only to my brother, Mordecai, but to your son, Aelfgar Athelwulfson."

It is difficult to say who was the most astounded, Aethelwulf or Aelfgar. There was a strange silence as they stared at each other and tried to take in the words that they had both just heard. Before either of them could speak there was a loud crashing sound followed by shouting and suddenly the two Normans from the boat came bursting into the room. They had their swords drawn and had positioned themselves so that they commanded the room. As always, the elder Norman seemed ready to explode with anger, but it was the younger one who spoke. He directed his words at Aelfgar.

"Right, you little shit, where is our letter? We know you have it. Neither the Captain nor the crew had it and it was nowhere on the boat. Give it to us."

Aelfgar looked at the Norman and for a moment saw his uncle before him and in an instant, defiant reaction he said

"No, never!"

With that the Norman lunged at Aelfgar but before his sword reached Aelfgar he found it being twisted from his grip by Aethelwulf. The Norman reacted quickly and was in the process of drawing his dagger from his belt when he was stabbed in the throat by his own sword. The other Norman grabbed Aelfgar from behind and holding his sword blade across Aelfgar's throat shouted in a clear calm voice

"Drop the sword or I'll cut the boy's throat!"

Aethelwulf stood very still and without lowering the sword looked directly into Aelfgar's eyes. In an instant Aelfgar knew what he had to do. He took a step backwards into the Norman whilst at the same time hooking his foot behind the Norman's then he pushed back with all his might. Both he and the Norman crashed to the ground and as they did, Aelfgar rolled away from the Norman's sword arm leaving the Norman exposed to Aethelwulf. The Norman was quick to recover and as Aethelwulf plunged his sword into the Norman's chest, the Norman drove his sword up into Aethelwulf's body. The Norman died instantly, and Aethelwulf fell to the floor unconscious and did not move.

Suddenly there was silence. The two Normans lay dead on the floor. Aelfgar, together with Avhram and Mordecai, rushed over to Aethelwulf. Gently taking his father's body in his arms Aelfgar stared down in disbelief. For years he had yearned to see his father again and he had travelled across land and sea to find him only to see him killed before they could speak to each other. He was overwhelmed with the feeling of being cheated. He wanted to scream and curse but instead he wiped some blood from the corner of Aethelwulf's mouth. As he did so Aethelwulf's eyes opened and seeing Aelfgar's face before him, he found some strength from somewhere and managed to smile.

"Aelfgar? Is it really you?"

"Yes, Father, it is me." Aethelwulf started coughing and blood began to trickle from the corner of his mouth once more.

"How did you find me? I had given up all hope of seeing you again."

"It is a long story Father, but mainly it was luck."

"You have grown so much since I last saw you. There is so much I want to tell you...." His face distorted as a sharp pain shot through his body.

"Father, rest for a moment."

Aethelwulf smiled again and forced himself to speak

"It means so much to see you again." His eyes now began to glaze over and without warning Aelfgar felt his father's life leave him. Aelfgar sat there holding his father, wishing him back to life. After a moment, Mordecai put a gentle arm around Aelfgar's shoulder and with Avhram's help they eased Aethelwulf away from Aelfgar's grip. They carried the body into a cooler part of the house with Aelfgar following still unable to believe that he had found his father only to see him killed with so much unsaid. Avhram and Mordecai laid Aethelwulf on a bed and covered him with a cotton sheet. Suddenly Aelfgar felt exhausted and slumped in the nearest chair. Mordecai sat quietly next to Aelfgar while Avhram went to fetch a drink of water. As Aelfgar sipped the cool water Avhram and Mordecai discussed what to do next. They decided that the local constable needed to be informed and then Aethelwulf and the bodies of the two Normans needed to be removed. Mordecai explained to Aelfgar that they were going to leave him for a while but would return shortly.

Stevie felt exhausted having been reading continuously for so long. Her tiredness and the unexpected twist of the sudden death of Aelfgar's father when they had only just been reunited made her feel very emotional. She thought about her father and how, since her rescue, they had managed to reconcile their differences. How devastated she would have been to have lost her father before they had the chance to do that together.

Chapter 7

Death and Rebirth

Aelfgar sat there alone and looked across at his father's body as it lay on the bed. In the end it did not matter that he still did not know why his father had never come back home to Maeldubesburg. What mattered was that it was clear his father had always loved him. As he sat there, Aelfgar thought about Ffraid, she did not know that her son had died. Then suddenly, in that moment, he could see into Ffraid's cottage and there, sitting by the fireside he could see Ffraid, Aunt Aemma and Rhiannon. Ffraid had her head in her hands and the other women were trying to comfort her. As he watched, Ffraid raised her head, and he could see she had been crying. So, she knew. Aelfgar also realised that she was aware of his presence. Aelfgar began to cry. He felt united with Ffraid in grief.

At that moment Avhram came back into the bedroom and Aelfgar lost concentration and Ffraid went from his mind. In his hand Avhram was carrying a scroll with broad ribbon around it. He stood silently before Aelfgar and waited until Aelfgar was ready to pay attention.

"Aelfgar, my boy, I am so sorry your father is dead. He and I had become good friends and he confided in me about his life and his later struggles. He lost his way completely after leaving you and was in the process of rebuilding his life. He thought about you a lot and desperately wanted to make amends for abandoning you. This is his journal in which he describes his personal journey since you last saw him. I know that he would want you to have it."

Aelfgar took the scroll from Avhram and immediately recognised the ribbon wrapped around the scroll. In fact, it was not a ribbon but a banner that Aelfgar had made from an old shirt for his father. Aelfgar had been eight years old at the time and had painstakingly copied Aethelwulf's emblem on to the strip of one of his old shirts using charcoal from the fire. Aethelwulf had been so pleased with his present and had promised Aelfgar that he would carry it with him always.

"Aelfgar. I have arranged for your father's body to be collected and prepared for cremation. Why don't you come with me to the side of the pool where you can sit in the shade and read your father's personal journal?"

Aelfgar was reluctant to leave his father's body, but he really did not want to see it removed as he knew it must be. So, he went with Avhram and found himself sitting on a bench in the shade looking across a sunlit courtyard, past the twinkling pool at a mural on the opposite wall. It was a painting of the Tree of Life exactly as he had seen it in his vision. Aelfgar felt that this was the perfect place for him to read his father's journal. He untied the banner from around the scroll and unrolling it, began to read. He did not recognise his father's writing, it seemed to be lacking his usual confidence. Aelfgar felt nervous as he began to read his father's words.

Lost, this is the first word that I need to write. I am far from home and trapped in a very dark and unforgiving place, my head. For a while now I have been caught up in a maelstrom of self-torment. My mind has been severely battered and bruised. My soul has been diminished and I am....... lost. The only thing that keeps me from disintegrating completely is the desperate need to make amends. This world into which I have fallen contains no reason or logic and no compassion. It is a world of stark recrimination. I am constantly tumbling around in a dark, deep pit, bouncing off the walls, bumping into the many things that I have done wrong in my life and into the chances I have missed to do the right thing. I never seem to be at a rest. For a long time now, I have been struggling with how to break this cycle and begin to climb out of this pit of despair. Some people in a similar situation might have turned to God for help. I have never been a religious believer. God was always for other people. The only person that I have ever believed in was me, myself, and now I have found out that I have built my belief on a flawed foundation. It has been suggested by Prince Nazim that I start writing this journal. His view is that until I face each of my errors and misdeeds one by one, I will never escape my personal hell. He also suggested that I address this journal to someone who would want to know what has happened to me. I am writing this for my son, Aelfgar. It is my hope that by describing my wasted life, I will be able to draw a line under my past and begin to build a new life. Perhaps by revisiting my past mistakes I can use them to find a way to put things right. Somehow, I need to restore the light.

How did I fall into this dark place? That is a question I have asked myself a hundred times. As I sit here trying to sort out the tumble of thoughts and memories that fill my mind, I need to find a way of organising my them. Looking back, I can start to see that my past can be divided into three periods. There is the main part that I might call my "innocent selfish period". This is before the point when self-doubt began to creep in. Sadly, this was for most of my lifetime. Then there is the next part that I could call "my doubt and denial period". The time when I battled with self-doubt for the first time in my life. Finally comes the part that I am in now, which I will call "my disintegration and reconstruction period". Yes, I can see that from a child until I met Brother Francisco, I lived only focussed on my selfish ambition. I lived in a self-satisfied state oblivious of the feelings of those around me. Then Brother Francisco started a period of increasing doubt in my way of viewing the world. This period ended on a battlefield in Sicily when, about to die, I was forced to admit to myself that I was a failure and that my life had been wasted. That should have been the end of it but miraculously I was saved, not by a member of my own side but by my enemy; by one of the very people that I was trying to slaughter! This act of mercy was the final straw. As I tried to come to terms with the fact that I was not going to die, that this life I had wasted was going to go on and that instead of being killed by my enemy I was going to be saved by him, I began to collapse mentally.

November 1068 – Aleppo

It has taken me a month to get back to my journal. I was pleased with myself after my first entry and went to discuss it with Prince Nazim, the man who saved me from death. He has since become my friend. The first friend I have ever had. He has stood by me during this dark period, providing me with food and shelter. More than that he has supported me in my quest to regain my mental balance. Over breakfast one day I read my journal to him. Having listened intently Prince Nazim asked me some questions which led me subsequently to a great deal of further soul searching. The first question he asked me was why I had used the word innocent in my phrase "innocent selfish time" and had not just said "selfish time". I could not give him an answer. He then asked me if I could remember how Brother Francisco caused me to have that first doubt and what it was. Again, I could not give him a clear answer. I went away and began trawling through my memory once more but this time with the purpose of being able to answer his questions. I concluded that I had used the word innocent to mean that while I was living life entirely driven by my selfishness, I was completely unaware of the negative impact of my actions on others and therefore was innocent of deliberately harming others. I know the effect was the same as if I had an evil purpose, but my guilt does not extend to my intent. I did many things that I now regret and need to address but I never did any of them meaning to do harm. When I gave Prince Nazim, this answer he then asked me if I felt that this distinction between innocent or evil purposes would mean anything to the people that I had harmed. Prince Nazim said this in his usual kind and caring manner. From that time on the battlefield, when he first displayed his charitable nature in saving me from certain death, he had consistently supported me in my recovery. So again, I had to think deeply and for a long time. I found this very hard. It has never been my nature to review and analyse my actions. My life and my decision making were carried out almost entirely at an unconscious instinctive level. This was the first time I had ever really tried to think things through in any kind of depth. As I replayed my life one more time, I began to realise that I had led my life totally unaware of the kindness and generosity that I had been shown by many people. Equally I had been blind to the manipulation and disadvantage that I had been subjected to by others. I then puzzled over how I had been unaware of these things at the time and yet I could be aware of them now as I trawled through my memories. This bothered me and I have spent many hours trying to find an answer.

Eventually, I concluded that there must be two people in my head and that from when I was a child, they have always been growing and developing in parallel inside me. There was one part of me, who was the dominating strong-willed person that everyone knew; but now I believe there must have been another hidden person; a gentler, kinder me, who was constantly being overridden by the first and who could only watch and record the wrongs being done by the first me. It seems to me that, in that moment on the battlefield when I realised that I was about to die having wasted my life, this second part of me had finally asserted itself. I feel sure that the dark period that followed was caused by it unleashing its pent-up anger and frustration at the previously dominant part of me. It was as if it had kept a detailed log of everything I had ever done and was now holding the unthinking me to account. As I sit here in Aleppo living in Prince Nazim's Palace replaying the events and decisions of my life, I am trying to let this gentler side of me express itself. I have tried to keep my mind open to its criticism and to accept it honestly. I am making a real effort to replace my arrogant pride with a newfound humility. It is with this frame of mind I have given some thought to Prince Nazim's questions.

If I go back to my very earliest memories, they are of being captivated by the old warriors and their tales of battles with the Vikings. Their pride in their heroic deeds and the esteem that they had within their group made a big impression on me. I became obsessed with emulating them. All I wanted was for tales to be told about me. I can see now that this obsession led to me treating those close to me badly, particularly my father. I could not recognise at the time that he had a different type of courage and prowess. The quiet kind of heroism required to establish a homestead for his extended family, to maintain the peace enabling everyone to flourish and grow. I now realise that he had always made his decisions by considering what was best for others. He measured his success by what he did for others and not what he achieved for himself. I am ashamed to say that until now I have been ignorant of the sacrifices that he made for me to be free to achieve my dreams. A lesser man would have used his authority as the head of the household and as my father, to put me in my place but he chose to be generous and big-hearted when I criticised him for not being a war hero. He just let my arrows of disdain bounce off his tough hide and allowed me to follow my own path. He must have seen me as a cocky, ungrateful self-absorbed child, but he must have loved me enough not to want to bring me down. He died when I was eighteen years old and will never know that I have finally come to appreciate him. I know if he were around now and saw my desperate state, he would not gloat at the fall from my self-established pedestal but would put his arm over my shoulder and say, "Let's go hunting".

Continuing my looking back, I must now face the way I treated my mother. After my father's death, I never thought once about my mother and that she would be grieving for my father. I never showed her any consideration. I was so focussed on becoming a King's Thegn and building a heroic reputation that I shoved aside anything that did not fit with my ambition. I allowed myself to see my mother as an impediment to achieving success. I dismissed her deep spiritual nature and Celtic culture as stupid superstitious nonsense. Even though I have never believed in a god of any kind, I had become a Christian to make myself more acceptable to King Edward. Because of this I felt that my mother needed to become a Christian too because I was sure King Edward would hold the fact that in his eyes she was a pagan against me. He could be difficult at times, especially where religion was concerned. Many people thought of him as a pious man but looking back on events, I would say he was narrow minded and intolerant. Anyway, the result was that I selfishly demanded that my mother give up everything that she believed in so I could further my ambition. She, of course, refused to and I saw her as just being deliberately awkward and in a fit of pique I banished her from her own home. I forbade her from seeing any of the family, especially you Aelfgar.

I now truly regret that I did this and wish I had taken the time to understand her beliefs and cultural heritage. I now feel that there was a lot about life that I might have learnt from her. It is unlikely that I will ever see her again but if I could, I would ask her forgiveness. In a different way, I was just as unfair on my younger brother Sigewulf. He was like my father, a quiet, down to earth man and like my father seemed to have a generosity that I have never possessed. After my father died and I became head of the household, I was so busy building my reputation and ingratiating myself with King Edward that quite naturally, and with no real discussion, Sigewulf stepped up to fill the void left by me and my preoccupation. He just started taking responsibility for the day to day running of our household and later, when I achieved my goal and became a King's Thegn, he did the same with the town of Maeldubesburg and surrounding area. I now realise that I was only free to live the life I wanted because I had a brother willing to relieve me of my responsibilities as head of the community. Sigewulf and his wife Aemma never complained about the absences and neglect of my duties. I hope they are prospering and continuing to care for you, Aelfgar They had no children of their own and willingly stepped in to take responsibility for bringing you up. Beatrice, your mother, never wanted children and certainly did not want anything to do with your day-to-day upbringing. When I think of you, I am sure that we had a good relationship because all I remember is happy times when we were together. I would return from one of my adventures and make a fuss of you and then disappear again. I think you were proud of me and would only have good memories too. I now realise that it is only because Sigewulf and Aemma gave you the a secure and reliable love that I had a solid foundation for my ephemeral visits. You must be a young man now and I regret that I did not spend more time with you. What would I say to you now Aelfgar? If I could see you again, I would tell you not to model yourself on the father that you remember but to to learn from my mistakes. I would tell you to listen to the voice inside you as it might save you from doing something you later regret. Finally, I would say whenever you get the chance to do something good for someone just do it. How I wish that I had done more for others instead of taking from them. I have taken liberties with everyone that loved me. I have taken opportunities to further my personal agenda whenever possible. I have even taken the lives of other warriors; after all that is what heroes do. I never did any of these things with evil intent, just from a position of wanting my own way. Of the many men I killed in combat, I never hated any of them as individuals or wished them any personal malice. Their deaths were the unfortunate consequence of my driving need to be a hero. I now regret all these things and would say to you Aelfgar "Open your eyes to those around you and take care of those who need your help. Avoid doing unintentional harm to anyone and avoid the company of self-interested people." I would go even further and say, "look for opportunities to give to everyone in some way or other, no matter how big or small." I hope that you have been generous with your mother as I never was. This I deeply regret. I married Beatrice de Beauville not because I loved her but because King Edward persuaded me to. He wanted to repay an old debt to his friend Sir Hugh de Beauville. Beatrice did not love me either. For her it was a convenient way to escape her family. Her mother had died when she was still a small child and both her father and brother ignored her. She retreated into a private world that became dominated by her relationship with God. When she was fourteen, she asked her father if she could become a nun. He refused partly out of spite but partly because he did not want to lose the possibility of marrying her off for political advantage one day. Whilst Beatrice was an attractive woman, she was quite cold with any potential suitors, preferring her own company rather than theirs. Eventually King Edward, who had become friends with Sir Hugh while he was in exile, decided to relieve his friend of his problem daughter. He suggested to me that if I wanted to become one of his Thegns, I should take a wife and that he could not think of anyone better than Beatrice. While Sir Hugh was happy to seize the chance to rid himself of Beatrice, he still drove a hard bargain when it came to paying any dowry. Ralph, Beatrice's brother, absolutely hated the idea of being connected by marriage to an Anglo-Saxon and made his views known. In private moments, Beatrice and I came to a personal agreement in which she agreed to bear me one child on the condition that she did not have to look after it and that I took the risk that the baby might not be a boy. On my part I agreed that if she had the one child then I would keep her as my wife but allow her to live her life unencumbered by worldly responsibilities. As I reflect on my marriage, I feel a sense of guilt that I coldly used Beatrice to provide me with a son and heir; you, Aelfgar. I could have taken the opportunity to have shown your mother some love and kindness for the first time in her life but instead I just ignored her just as her father and brother had done. Sitting here now and thinking about this period, the matter that fills me with the greatest shame is the fact that at the time I was so satisfied with myself. I was so pleased with my progress in fulfilling my vision of becoming a famous hero. At the same time I was completely blind to the effect of my behaviour on others.

Getting back to Prince Nazim's questions. Did it make a difference to the people that I had harmed that my actions had no evil intention? I think to the people that loved and cared for me it did make a difference. It allowed them to forgive me and be generous in accepting my selfishness because they knew that any harm that they received was unintentional. For everyone else it made no difference at all. Having given it a lot of thought I think a better word to use, rather than "innocent" is "ignorant". I told Prince Nazim this and he nodded his agreement.

Later, I also answered his questions about when and how self-doubt crept into my life and started to chew away at my sanity. There was no sign of my future collapse when I left Maeldubesburg for the last time. I arrived in Lunden and went to see King Edward who had sent for me. The King was an intimidating man. Physically he was very tall with a full head of white hair and a matching beard. Because of his height he tended to stoop a little which caused him to look with slightly downcast eyes and those who did not know him could be forgiven for seeing him as a humble man. He was in fact a crafty, wily man who liked to get his own way. At this time, I was in awe of him and saw him as a wise and clever King whom I wanted to please and to have him think good of me. When he gave me my assignment, I had no doubts about why he was sending me to Rome with the Archbishop of Cantwaraburh. It was because I was his loyal Thegn, capable and respected. Now, however, I realise he was as self-interested as I was and had used my desire to achieve greatness to manipulate me into serving his needs. As I have already made clear, the old, proud side of me was oblivious to what other people were thinking or feeling. All my senses were totally focussed on my own thoughts and feelings; I was not at all interested or aware of the people around me. This not only left me dependent on the goodwill of others but vulnerable to those who wanted to use me for their own ends. It never occurred to me that the King was about to reward my loyalty to him with an act of deliberate personal betrayal, or that this act would lead to the collapse of my world to the brink of complete destruction. No, at the time, my world was completely untouched by any doubt. The first uncertainty that penetrated my self-built fortress of ignorance was placed there by Brother Francisco di Santiago during our journey from Cantwaraburh to

Rome on the Via Francigena. He had joined our group as we were leaving Cantwaraburh. He was travelling to Rome on a pilgrimage alone and asked to travel with us under our protection. We, of course, welcomed him in our party. Brother Francisco's very first words to me were to ask why was I travelling with the Devil incarnate? When I replied that I did not know what he was talking about, he responded with another question. He asked me whether I thought it was right that the head of the Christian church in England should be the richest person in the land. When I answered that I had never thought about it, he said that I should. He felt that I should compare the Archbishop's life to the life of the man he was representing, Jesus Christ. As the journey progressed Brother Francisco plagued us all with his unsolicited and pointed questions. Eventually, the Archbishop insisted that Thurstan, the Archbishop's bodyguard, and I ride apart from the rest of the group and keep Brother Francisco with us, by force if necessary. This saved the others from Brother Francisco's continual interrogation but meant that Thurstan and I became the focus of Brother Francisco's attention. He was different from any man I had ever met. Physically he was quite ordinary, smaller than most men and dark in complexion. His most noticeable feature was his eyes. They were hooded which made them seemed to be half closed. They had the menace of a bird of prey awaiting the right moment to pounce. When Brother Francisco pounced it was usually with a penetrating question, delivered in a calm, intense manner. If Brother Francisco were a sword-thrust, he would not be a wild slashing cut or violent and savage lunge but a silent sword-point slowly and relentlessly piercing the throat of its victim. But it was not his appearance that made him different; it was his unshakeable belief in Jesus Christ and that Jesus Christ had been betrayed by the Church, who used his story to achieve power over others. He felt that they had twisted Jesus's messages to place the Church between people and God. They had taken Jesus's loving generosity and perverted it so they could establish an authoritative controlling organisation and create power and wealth for themselves. He believed that Jesus was born to serve every human-being alive and that Jesus possessed an all-encompassing and totally unconditional love for everyone. He also believed that because Jesus was a man and not a God, he had also possessed passion and desire. His direct challenges had upset the established Jewish religion of the time who were using their religion to achieve power and privilege over ordinary people. Brother Francisco had chosen early on in his life to try and emulate Jesus and challenge the power and authority of the Church. He knew he was risking his life in doing so. He was not just a rebel like Jesus. He also cared, as Jesus had, about saving people's souls. He seemed to have made up his mind that Thurstan and I needed to have our souls saved and the journey to Rome gave him the opportunity to do so. One day, as we started the long climb towards the pass through the high mountains Brother Francisco asked me the question that opened a tiny crack in my armour of self-satisfaction. He asked if I believed in Jesus and I replied dismissively, that of course I did, even though I did not. Then Brother Francisco questioned how my belief in Jesus affected the way I lived my life. I replied that I did not understand what he meant. Brother Francisco fixed me with his hooded stare and rather issuing another question, as he usually did, he explained what Jesus meant to him and how his belief in Jesus affected the way he behaved. He believed that Jesus had been sent by God to serve the whole of mankind and help them to find God for themselves. As John the Baptist had proclaimed, Jesus was the Messiah come to erase the sins that stood between the people and God. These sins were lust, gluttony, greed, sloth, wrath, envy, and pride. Brother Francisco did not believe in original sin. It was invented by the Church hundreds of years after Jesus's death. Brother Francisco believed that Jesus and John the Baptist showed the way to behave by serving others even if, as in the case of both Jesus and John the Baptist, it led to their death. Brother Francisco went on to explain his criticism of the Archbishop of Cantwaraburh; his wealth, his lack of generosity and his use of his position in the Church to gain even more benefits for himself. Father Francisco explained that he believed that if Jesus was amongst us on our journey, he would challenge everyone, including the Archbishop. He would ask them to examine themselves, to recognise their sins and to then approach God and ask for forgiveness. Father Francisco said he believed that as Jesus was not among us, it was his duty to act in Jesus's place. He then returned his focus to me and asked again how my knowledge of Jesus affected the way I behaved. At this point I became fed up with his attention and brusquely answered that I did not know as I had never thought about it. I then kicked my horse on and rode ahead with his parting comment echoing around my head. "Well, you should think about it!" I tried not to, but I could not help it. My first thoughts were about why I had said that I believed in Jesus when I never have. I decided that I was continuing to live the lie that had enabled me to pretend to King Edward that I was religious and therefore worthy of being a King's Thegn. I perhaps could believe that Jesus had existed as a man, but I found the stories of his life and death to be irrelevant to me and my life. However, I did become fascinated with Brother Francisco. He was the first person, other than myself, that I ever really gave any thought to. I could not understand his motivation. I could not see what he stood to gain from acting as everyone's conscience. Take Thurstan for instance. Brother Francisco was equally relentless in pressing Thurstan as to whether he believed in God and Jesus. Eventually, Thurstan admitted that he used to believe in God but not anymore. Brother Francisco was genuinely upset that Thurstan was heading for hell and made it his responsibility to save him. For my point of view, I did not care one bit about Thurstan heading for eternal damnation, partly because I was not convinced that hell existed, but mainly because I did not care what happened to Thurstan or anybody, other than me. As far as I was concerned, it was up to him to save himself. Thurstan tried hard to avoid answering Brother Francisco's questions about what had caused his loss of faith but eventually he caved in and one evening as we sat around our campfire not far from the main camp, he told us his story. He had only been the Archbishop's bodyguard for a few months when he was required to accompany the Archbishop to Eoforwic. The purpose of the visit was a meeting between the two Archbishops of Cantwaraburh and Eoforwic to discuss some pressing theological problems raised by King Edward regarding his vow of pilgrimage to St

Peter's tomb in Rome and his subsequent inability to fulfil his vow. Thurstan's wife was in the final days of pregnancy and could not travel so stayed at home in Saedingburgha not far from Cantwaraburh. At this time Thurstan was a practising Christian and he attended a service of blessing that was held by the archbishop. Its purpose was to bless the journey to Eoforwic and to protect the members of the archbishop's entourage. Thurstan asked to have his wife and unborn child included in the blessing even though she was staying behind. This was granted. The meeting in Eoforwic lasted longer than planned so it was nearly a month before Thurstan returned to Saedingburgha to see his wife and new-born child. He knew something was wrong when he entered his homestead; for his father was waiting for him by the main gate. Thurstan learnt that shortly after his departure his wife had gone into labour and there had been complications and both she and her baby had died. Thurstan was devastated and could not understand why God had allowed this to happen, especially as the Archbishop had prayed for their protection. Why would God allow this to happen to two such innocents who had never done a thing to harm anyone? This inability to understand led him to become bitter towards God. What was the point of worshipping someone who had ignored the prayers of one of his representatives on earth and had not extended any protection when it was needed? From that point onwards, Thurstan ignored God as God had ignored the archbishop. Brother Francisco said he was sad to hear of Thurstan's loss and even sadder that it had caused the loss of Thurstan's faith. Brother Francisco tried to tell Thurstan that God had a reason for his wife and child's death and that even though we cannot understand we must trust that it was for the good. The look on Thurstan's face said he was not in any way convinced by this argument, and I am sure my own face conveyed the same. I realise now that this is what the word "faith" means; to believe without proof or evidence. Brother Francisco had faith and he really believed that God had a purpose for the death of Thurstan's wife and child and he was determined to help Thurstan rediscover his faith and be at peace. I felt no such need to help ease Thurstan's pain and I found it hard to understand why Brother Francisco felt the need to do so. This led to me asking the first question I had ever asked to understand another person. I asked Brother Francisco why he cared that Thurstan refound his faith and his answer was he cared because God cared. He said he was convinced that God wanted him to give himself to helping others in any way he could. He then turned back to me and asked me what he could do to help me overcome my pride and reach out to God. As I told Prince Nazim, this is how doubt had entered my world. I started to question why I, unlike Brother Francisco, had never felt any need to help anyone I have ever met, including my own family.

However, it was only when we got to Rome that this initial tiny crack in my self-assurance was forced open by the events that took place there.

The archbishop was immediately granted a private audience with the Pope when we arrived in Rome. Thurstan, Brother Francisco and I had gone with the archbishop and were required to wait in an outer chamber. The doors to the Pope's chamber were guarded by four burly Lombards, two of whom had taken our weapons on our arrival. After a while, the doors opened, and the Pope's secretary summoned Brother Francisco into the Pope's chamber. The vast doors were closed behind them. Shortly afterwards, despite the thickness of the large wooden doors, Thurstan and I could hear shouting which seemed to last a long time before terminating with a shriek. The doors then flew open and out came two more guards carrying an unconscious Brother Francisco. We stared in disbelief, as he was dragged away down some nearby stairs. Before we had a chance to react, the archbishop appeared and spoke to us. His manner was terse and irritated. First, he focussed his attention on me.

"Aethelwulf, I want to remind you that you are a King's Thegn and that you have sworn to do the King's bidding without hesitation or question." It was now my turn to be irritated.

"Archbishop, there is no call for you to say that. I have never wavered in my obedience to the King's wishes. He has been and will always be the reason that I live." He nodded and reached inside his robes and extracted a rolled parchment which he handed to me. I could see the King's seal upon it.

"Please open and read these orders from the King. Hurry, the Pope is awaiting my return." I read the contents and found out that I was ordered by the King to obey the Archbishop's orders as if they were his own." It did not make sense. I was the Kings Thegn, not the Archbishop's; that was Thurstan's responsibility. Before I could say anything, the Archbishop turned his attention to Thurstan.

"Thurstan, when you swore your loyalty to me as my vassal, you promised to obey my every command. I am going to give both you and Aethelwulf a set of orders that, for the Kings wellbeing and mine, you must both obey. Many years ago, in return for the Pope's support in claiming the throne of England, King Edward promised the Pope that he would make a pilgrimage to Rome in gratitude. That has not happened and the King has sent me here to negotiate a pardon for this omission so that he can avoid eternal damnation. A moment ago, I presented an alternative offer from the King to build a church in London dedicated to Saint Peter. But, as King Edward predicted, it was not sufficient to satisfy his Holiness. Consequently, I presented the King's additional offer which was to provide the services of two of his most valiant and dedicated warriors to his Holiness's army for a period of five years to aid in the fight against the Muslim army in Sicily. His Holiness has accepted this improved offer and issued an indulgence absolving the King of all his sins, including his failure to make his promised pilgrimage. This leads me to your new orders. You are both to accompany me to swear your allegiance to his Holiness and to receive his blessing before joining his army in Southern Italy."

Aelfgar, the sense of betrayal I felt towards my King was overwhelming. To be bartered by him to achieve his personal ambitions with complete disregard to my own ambitions and desires hurt my pride more than I will ever be able describe. I could see that Thurstan felt the same way about the Archbishop, having served him faithfully without question. We had the same dilemma. We were both honourable men bound by our code of loyalty to stay true to our vows and promises and yet to do so meant we allowed ourselves to be traded into the service of another. Having no time to think we were swept along by the schemes of others and this is how I ended up facing an inglorious death in Sicily. As I write about this betrayal, I realise that it must have dented my pride so much that what subsequently happened to Brother Francisco was able to penetrate my shell of self-importance and undermine my self-confidence. We found out that earlier when the Archbishop was in his audience with the Pope, he had reported Brother Francisco as a heretic. When summoned and confronted with this charge, Brother Francisco lectured the Pope on his abuse of the words of Jesus and for using them to achieve power over the common people who only sought love and understanding. Of course, he was taken to the cells, found guilty of heresy and sentenced to death. By coincidence, as Thurstan and I left Rome with the Pope's army, we passed through the square where Brother Francisco was about to be burnt at the stake. We both felt uncomfortable as we passed by him. He seemed quite calm and serene until he saw us. To our surprise rather calling for our help, he started pleading with us to honour his death by turning to Jesus for help to save our souls. Clearly, we could not stop or even slow down, so we were swept along with the rest of the army to the sound of Brother Francisco begging us to save our souls. For the rest of our journey, I puzzled over why Brother Francisco consistently put the spiritual welfare of others above his own. Why, even as he prepared to die, did he want to save the souls of others? Even when I was alone on the battlefield and all I could think about was saving myself from death, that question appeared in my mind. Of course, now I know it was because it was his purpose in life.

December 1068 Aleppo

So here I am sitting in the orchard in Prince Nazim's garden and I have finally finished making my confessions and counting my past wrongs. Where do I go from here? I have managed to drag myself out of my pit of self-recrimination and now must prevent myself falling back. To do this, I need to find a way to make amends for my past by doing something for others with what is left of my life. But what? I am starting from nowhere. I am nobody, I have lost my swagger, my unthinking certainty. I lack confidence and have no idea where to start. Prince Nazim suggests that, rather than searching intellectually for some grand scheme that will turn my life around, I should just start doing good deeds with no expectation of reward or gratitude. He says that I am like a man standing before a rope bridge over a deep chasm. I can stand and look, think about how challenging it is, but unless I take the first step, I will remain stranded on this side of the chasm. Prince Nazim also suggested that I try to let the previously neglected and quieter side of me tell me what to do next. This will mean subduing the old dominant me and waiting for the new me to speak.

January 1069 Aleppo

One morning a few days later, I went out of the Palace for the first time since my arrival. I was dressed in plain clothes and wandered around Aleppo mixing with the inhabitants who were going about their daily business. I tr stopped myself having a plan or objective and I just observed. I found it to be quite satisfying watching the little interactions between people and seeing daily life as I had never seen it before. After about an hour or two I was near the edge of town walking down a steep lane that led back to the market. In the distance, coming towards me, was an elderly lady carrying a large basket full of produce that she had bought in the town. It was clear as I watched her that carrying such a heavy load up the hill was a struggle for her and was beginning to cause her distress. Instantly I knew that I should help her and acting immediately, I approached her and using sign language offered to carry the basket up the hill for her. At first, she looked at me suspiciously but then smiled and handed me her basket. We did not speak as we walked up the hill and when we got to the top, she took her basket back and turned down a side alley and was gone. I stood alone at the top of the hill and for the first time in a long time, smiled. I had taken my first step.

March 1069 Aleppo

Over the next few months, I went out into the town regularly and allowed opportunities to present themselves to me. I would respond by doing some little kindness. Then one day Prince Nazim came to me as I sat in my favourite spot here in the orchard and asked if I would do him a small favour. I, of course, said yes straight away. I could not let the chance to repay my friend, my mentor and saviour pass, even if only in a small way. He asked me if I would be willing to personally deliver a letter to his sister who was living in a town called Tunis in Ifriqiya. It would mean travelling to the coast and getting a boat along the Mediterranean coast. I immediately felt anxious. It seemed a big step to leave the comfort of Aleppo's city walls and the prince's palace. I felt an internal conflict going on between my desire to repay the prince's kindness to me and my fear of facing the wider world. The prince in his wisdom had expected this and remained silent while I battled to resolve my opposing feelings. I tried to open my mind to my new self and heard its voice say, "You know what you should do." I told the prince it would be my honour to take his letter and deliver it in person to his sister in Tunis.

As the boat that I was travelling on followed the coastline of Ifriqiya towards Tunis, I could feel my anxiety begin to well up. In my previous life I had faced the fiercest opponents in mortal combat and felt no fear or unease and now, I seemed to be scared by something that I could not see or describe. It was a strange feeling to be without the confidence that had previously existed. Perhaps I will never return to such supreme confidence again as I now know it was built on an equally supreme level of ignorance. Prince Nazim had accompanied me to the dockside to wish me well on the journey and to pass over the letter for his sister. His parting words now rang in my head.

"Aethelwulf, my dear friend, the time has come to start trusting yourself again and let the new you guide your thoughts and actions. You must trust that now it has made itself known to you it will not go away or let the old you return. It is stronger than you think." So as the boat slowed down as it approached the moorings, I tried to tell myself to relax and let the future before me happen without worrying. Once I was ashore, I followed Prince Nazim's instructions and went straight to the gates of the Emir's palace. As I walked slowly through the town, I looked around me taking in the sights and sounds of the city. I was dressed in a grey set of robes and, despite my height, I drew no attention from the people around me, for which I was grateful. I presented a letter of introduction from the prince to the guards on the gates and was courteously but firmly requested to wait on a stone bench a short way along the inside of the gatehouse wall. After about an hour a group of people appeared through the inner doorway of the gatehouse. Leading the group was a strikingly beautiful woman dressed in plain robes of deep blue and a simple head scarf of dark green.

The understated nature of her clothing seemed to emphasise the beauty of her features, especially her dark sparkling eyes. The woman wore a smile that would have softened the hardest of hearts. With her was an equally beautiful woman but of a complete contrast in appearance. Her hair, which was uncovered and flowing freely, was the colour of pale gold with the softest of curls. Her eyes were bright blue and her complexion was of pale white marble. Also accompanying the women were two soldiers who seemed relaxed but at the ready. The leading woman spoke and her voice matched her appearance, being serene and confident.

"I am A'isha al-Hurra, Prince Nazim's sister. Welcome to Tunis, Aethelwulf. I am so happy that my brother has sent you to visit me. I long to hear news of him and how he is faring. First, let me introduce my companion. Aethelwulf, this is Lady Elouise. She is a guest of the Emir and I have been given the responsibility of caring for her." I looked at the golden lady that I had just been introduced to and from the moment that our eyes met, I felt that I had known her all my life. From the way she smiled at me I sensed that she had felt something similar.

"It is a pleasure to meet you" I said, hoping that I sounded more confident than I felt. Up until then we had all been speaking in Latin but when the golden lady spoke it was in French.

"Sir, I am pleased to meet you too. I know your name. You are a Saxon warrior who is quite famous in Normandy where I was born and where I spent most of my life." I was shocked as I had hoped to have left my past life behind and did not expect it to ever resurface again. I managed to suppress my consternation and replied.

"Ah Madam, I am a different person to that Aethelwulf; he died in Sicily." She smiled.

"Yet you look like a warrior." Now I smiled and replied

"That is probably the only similarity." At this point Princess A'isha spoke, again in Latin.

"Please, I am forgetting my manners. You have had a long journey. Come in out of the heat. We will all have plenty of time to talk once you have rested and eaten. I will also introduce you to the Emir. He is very keen to meet you."

Later, after meeting the Emir, a kind and friendly man, I had the opportunity to spend some time with Princess A'isha. As soon as we were alone, I fulfilled my promise to Prince Nazim.

"Princess A'isha, Prince Nazim sends you his fondest wishes and hopes you are well and asked me to give you this letter."

She smiled as she tucked the letter into a pocket in her robes and looking directly at me, asked me not to call her Princess as she had dropped that title when she became a doctor. However, I realised that my respect for Prince Nazim and my insecurity made it impossible to call her just A'isha as she had requested, so we came to an agreement. When we were alone, I would call her Princess but when anyone else was present I would call her my lady. I quickly found that she had a sharp sense of humour and liked to laugh. She told me that Prince Nazim was like a father to her even though he was only five years older. Their parents had died in an accident when she was young and Nazim became ruler while he was still a boy. He was given an "Elder Brother", who was selected for his wisdom and lack of personal ambition and with his help the prince had grown into a wise and just man. Prince Nazim had always taken care of his sister, helping her to grow and develop into a very capable person who had chosen to become a doctor. Suddenly she stopped speaking and apologised because she could no longer contain her desire to read her brother's letter and asked if I would leave her alone for a while. She rang a bell and one of her servants arrived immediately and on her instructions, he escorted me to the palace gardens to wait. I found a comfortable looking seat and sat down. The garden was a beautiful, tranquil place filled with bird song and the fragrance of many varieties of flowers. Yet now that I was by myself, I began to feel anxious and unsettled. I struggled to understand why I felt this way. After all, everything had gone smoothly since my arrival and everyone had treated me kindly. My restlessness began to overwhelm me, so I stood up and began to stroll around the garden. It was laid out in a geometric pattern with raised flower beds and avenues of orange trees. As I turned a corner into a side avenue I saw, walking towards me, the Lady Elouise. She was dressed in pale blue robes with a hood which covered her golden hair. As soon as she saw me, she broke into a smile.

"Ahh, it's the other Aethelwulf" she said softly and then looking around her, she continued.

"Isn't this a beautiful place and so vast. Did you know that beyond the stream and through the palm trees the Emir has a small zoo full of wild animals." There was something about her voice that had a calming effect on my anxiety, and I found myself beginning to relax.

"No, I didn't know that. I have only just started to explore this amazing garden." I found myself smiling back as I spoke. It occurred to me that I should smile more often as it made me feel better about myself. Then I noticed a cheeky twinkle appear in her clear blue eye and she offered to give me a guided tour of the garden. I, of course, accepted. After a period of strolling and small talk, she stopped, and removing her hood, she turned and looked me directly in the eye.

"You are the Aethelwulf that I heard about in my childhood, aren't you?" I could see her penetrating stare scanning my face for signs of my reaction. Maybe it was because I was feeling relaxed, maybe it was this strange feeling that we already knew each other or possibly because I needed to tell someone other than Prince Nazim, but I found myself answering her honestly.

"Lady Elouise, the answer is both yes and no. Yes, my body is the same body as that of the Aethelwulf that you have heard about but the person inside is not. The old Aethelwulf did die in Sicily and the Aethelwulf that you are talking to now was born in Aleppo shortly afterwards." She continued to study my face for a while then looking around, she saw a bench under a nearby olive tree and indicated for us to sit. Then in the most caring and natural way she took my hand in hers and with a gentle smile she said,

"I would very much like to know more, would you like to tell me what happened?" Unbelievably I found myself telling her my life story. All the time I was speaking she held my hand and listened intently. I did not hold back in explaining my shame at my past behaviour, my desire to make amends, my current lack of confidence and associated feelings of anxiety. When I had finished, she said quietly and sincerely

"Aethelwulf you were a great man, you will always be a great man. You cannot hide from your greatness!" I admit that part of me wanted to believe her, but another part found that an uncomfortable thought.

"That is kind of you to say but I cannot agree. My greatness before came from doing things so that other people admired me and praised me and that is exactly what led to my descent into the pit of self-loathing." She let go of my hand and brushed a wisp of hair from across her eyes.

"I don't believe that will happen again. From what you have said you are now driven by the desire to carry out acts of goodness for others. Your deeds will be great, not you." I smiled

"You mean well but I do not yet trust myself not to return to my old self-centred and self-important ways." With that, she stood suddenly

"Come, I have something to show you." We walked through the palm trees and entered a group of small buildings. The Lady Elouise strode purposefully towards one of the larger buildings. Inside this building was a cage and inside the cage was a powerful looking animal. I had never seen such a magnificent animal. It was a cat but bigger and more powerful than I have ever seen. It was burnt orange in colour with stripes of white and black randomly dispersed over its body. As we approached, the cat turned its head and stared at us with a disinterested look. Its jaw was slightly open to show a set of fearsome teeth and its tongue hung loosely out the side of its mouth. The animal prowled restlessly from one end of the cage to the other, going back and forth continuously. It seemed to be lost in its own world and not at all interested in us. The Lady Elouise moved away from me and approached the cage door and turned the key left in the lock. She then began to open the door slowly. The animal continued striding back and forth barely taking any notice of her. Eventually the door was wide open, and the Lady Elouise returned to my side. The animal kept up its relentless prowling for quite some time before stopping in front of the open door. I began to back away, but the Lady Elouise placed her hand on my arm to stop me.

"Watch" she whispered. The animal seemed uneasy and nervous and took a pace slowly towards the threshold. It stopped and tensed, as if about to spring and it lowered its head and started backing away. Then, as if nothing had happened, it recommenced its pacing back and forwards. After watching for a while, the Lady Elouise stepped forward, closed the door and relocked it.

"Come, let us return to the garden" she said linking her arm through mine. This small but familiar gesture reinforced in me the feeling that we had always known each other. Outside, as we strolled, Lady Elouise turned her gaze towards me once again and said.

"That magnificent animal is a Tiger, it lives in a land far to the east from here and in its natural world it is king. It is capable of fighting and defeating all other animals living around. It is quite capable of overcoming the pair of us if it wished. However, it has been locked in that cage for so long that it is comfortable there. It gets fed twice a day and faces no challenges as it grows older. You saw how it began to feel uncomfortable as it approached the door and how it hesitated to step into the unknown. You, Aethelwulf, are like that creature. You are trapped in your past and even though the door is open to a new life, you find it too discomforting to trust yourself and step through." She smiled and waited. Before I could reply, Princess A'isha appeared and came bounding towards us.

"Good, you have found each other. Aethelwulf, don't you just love this garden. I love spending time here. So, what did you two find to talk about?" While I was trying to decide what to say Lady Elouise answered.

"Nothing and everything. We strolled around and have just been visiting the zoo." I looked at Lady Elouise with a thank you in my eyes and she responded with a warm smile. Princess A'isha turned to me and spoke.

"Aethelwulf, I am so grateful to you for bringing my brother's letter to me. Reading it has made me extremely happy. Thank you for making sure it got to me. Forgive me for asking but I am curious Aethelwulf as to what you intend to do next. Will you return to Aleppo or stay here for a while or perhaps return to your homeland?" Still in a mood of openness and honesty I replied

"My Lady, in truth I do not know. I admit that going back to Aleppo appeals to me because I could live a comfortable life there. Staying here would be comfortable but I would feel like I was hiding away from life. Going back home has too many complications. I would really like to see my son Aelfgar again, but it would be difficult for me not fall back into my old ways. I feel strongly that my destiny lies elsewhere but I do not know where that might be. I have some things that I need to achieve before I can become truly content with myself and that probably means taking some risks." As I said this, I looked towards Lady Elouise who tilted her head sideways in silent acknowledgement. When I turned back towards Princess A'isha, she was looking at me in a way that I could not interpret but made me feel the Prince Nazim had perhaps said something about my history in his letter. Suddenly, Princess A'isha became agitated.

"Lady Elouise, I have been remiss and forgotten to tell you that the Emir would like to see you immediately. He is waiting for you by the Reflecting Pool in his private garden. I am sorry I did not tell as soon as I saw you." Lady Elouise smiled at the Princess with the same warmth that she had shown me earlier.

"What would the Emir want with me?" she said distractedly. Princess A'isha laughed

"Well, there is one way you can find out. Now run along."

When we were alone, Princess A'isha slipped her arm through mine, just as Lady Elouise had done earlier and began to stroll around the garden leading me towards the sound of running water. Shortly, we arrived at a sparkling pool with a fountain trickling water into the far end of the pool. We sat down on a stone bench and watched a small, colourful bird fly down and take a drink from the edge of the pool. After a while, Princess A'isha turned towards me.

"I am so glad that you have had a chance to get to know Lady Elouise better. What did you make of her?" I thought for a while before answering as I wanted to be sure that I could express myself accurately.

"She seems kind and thoughtful. I like her. I feel that I have known her for a long time even though I have only just met her. I cannot explain it. It makes no sense."

Princess A'isha gave a snort

"Aha, that is exactly what I feel. To me, she is like the sister that I have always wanted."

Out of nowhere, it suddenly struck me how much I had changed since my mental collapse. Here I was sitting quietly enjoying talking to someone about something other than myself and my personal ambitions. More than that, I was actively interested in someone else. I also realised that I felt completely comfortable speaking to the Princess. It is true to say that I have not had a lot of experience talking one to one with women. I allowed this newfound curiosity to have its way and decided to ask her about Lady Elouise. How did she come to be here in the Emir's palace? Who was she and what was going to happen to her? The Princess seemed to be happy to answer my questions. Lady Elouise was from Rouen in Normandy and was a descendent of the Viking King Rollo of Normandy. She had been promised by her father to the son of a Norman Duke when just a young girl. Last year she had become of an age to marry and was recently travelling by sea to Southern Italy to join her future husband. The ship that was carrying her was captured by pirates and she was taken hostage. However, before they could demand a ransom for her, the pirates were captured by one of the Emir's ships and she was rescued. The Emir was keeping her safe until it could be organised for her to safely continue her journey; hopefully, that will be quite

soon now. Having had my newfound curiosity satisfied, I switched my attention to the Princess. She seemed to be quite happy to sit and talk to me and so I decided to ask her about herself. She again responded positively and seemed pleased that I had asked. For a moment, I again wondered if Prince Nazim had told her about my troubles. She told me how as a young girl she had been drawn to the idea of helping sick people to get better. This, eventually, led to her studying medicine in Aleppo. It turned out that she had a bright mind and a natural gift for healing and her teachers recommended that she continue her studies at the hospital school in Kairouan, not far from where we were sitting. Whilst there, she came to the notice of the Emir's wife and after qualifying, she was appointed one of the palace doctors. She had now been here for three years and found the position very satisfying. As I looked at her and I saw how motivated she was about helping others get well, I took a chance and told her of my personal disintegration. I also told her that, with her brother's help I was trying to recover my identity and self-respect by finding a way to make amends for my past selfishness. Immediately, the doctor in her took over and holding my hand in hers, looking directly into my eyes, she asked me how I thought my recovery was progressing. I, again, thought hard before giving my answer.

"I feel that I have made the first hesitant steps in the right direction but have not yet made enough ground to say I was well on the way to making even a partial recovery." At this point another colourful bird flew down to the water's edge for a drink and we both sat silently watching until it flew off again.

"Aethelwulf, what is the progress that you have made so far?"

"In Aleppo, thanks to your brother's advice I was able to begin turning my attention away from my own concerns and towards the people around me and their concerns. I have begun to manage my anxiety and worry. Strangely, when talking to both you and Lady Elouise, I have felt calm and confident for the first time since my collapse, but I cannot tell you why." As I sat there, the thought struck me that, because the Princess was so intently focused on me and my well-being, she had lost all awareness of herself. This was something I wanted to be able to do myself someday. Keeping her voice hushed to match our surroundings she said.

"Those are good first steps. What do you feel you need to achieve as your next steps?" This time it was me that gave a snort.

"Right now, I have no idea other than I must not let myself take a step backwards. I would feel happier with myself if I could lock those small changes in place before moving on." The Princess gently let go of my hand and stood up. She started to walk slowly to and fro, reminding me of the tiger I saw earlier. After a while, she sat down again and placed her hand on top of mine.

"Aethelwulf, I can understand your uncertainty and your fear, but you must take heart from two things. Firstly, you have progressed a long way from the person my brother rescued from the battlefield and secondly, you now know what is right and wrong where you were ignorant before. Why not allow yourself to believe that the change is here to stay and you will never go back to the old you. For what it is worth I believe that you are already past the point of no return."

"Thank you, Princess; your observations really help. You have given me a lot to think about."

Later, when I was back in the room provided for me by the Emir, I stood looking out beyond the palace walls towards the sea. I thought about the fact that I had just opened my heart to two women who I had only just met. This would not have happened in the past. I also realised that showing my frailties was a good thing and had led to generosity and support from strangers. Thinking back to the conversation with the Princess earlier caused me to recall the first time I had met Prince Nazim, when I was fighting for the Christian army in Sicily. I had been separated from my comrades during a major battle. I had spent the previous evening fighting for my life and on the day in question I was alone on the battlefield and stood on a small mound surrounded by a sea of enemy soldiers. As the sun warmed the bodies at my feet, the awful stench of the previous day returned but to be honest, I did not care. I became aware that my enemies who had been camped around me, were beginning to stir. I could hear their groans as they awoke to find themselves still in the bad dream that they had hoped would fade with the dark. Their groans turned to angry shouts,and they started cursing as they saw their fellow soldiers lying dead at my feet while I waited to take more of their lives. Someone shouted an order and they moved towards me from all sides. By now I was so exhausted I was not capable of conscious thought but as an automatic response I set my shoulders, adjusted my stance, and brought my sword up into the guard position. Yesterday I had been invincible, killing at will. None of the enemy came anywhere near close to harming me, none of the arrows had got past my shield but I knew today would be different as I had not had anything to eat or drink since the previous day. I had not slept as I had had to stand ready all night just in case they rushed me during the darkness. So, as I stood ready, I began to accept that I was about to die. I had lived my entire life wanting to be a hero, but I now had to face the fact that this was not going to happen and I was about to die having achieved nothing. No-one back home would ever know that I was dead, and no-one would tell tales about my bravery or sing songs in praise of my heroic actions. Then, as the circle of soldiers closed around me, I became aware of the sound of horses being ridden hard and coming in my direction. Looking over the heads of the soldiers I could see a group of horses galloping towards us. The soldiers turned to see who it was and there was a look of astonishment on their faces as they dropped to their knees. There was an eerie silence as the leading rider dismounted from his horse. He was magnificently dressed. On his head was a golden helmet swathed in a purple turban that had a loose end which was wrapped around his throat. Across his shoulders he wore a vivid blue cloak. He also wore a gold embroidered jacket and a green and gold pair of trousers. He strode confidently through the ring of men, arriving directly in front of me where he slowly surveyed the scene. He then looked me directly in the eye and spoke to the men in Arabic with a strong and firm voice. Immediately the men retreated a considerable distance before placing their weapons on the ground before them. I was unsure what was happening. This finely attired man and I stood alone still staring into each other's eyes when his face broke into a broad grin and speaking in perfect French he said.

"I think you have killed enough of my men. Why don't you lower your sword and come with me?"

At this point, I was having difficulty focusing on his words and must have appeared reluctant, for he then said

"At some time my men will kill you. Do you really want to die here all alone? To be left to rot with no-one caring about your fate. Please, if you come with me, I promise that you will not be harmed."

I was still unsure of what was happening and was certainly not willing to trust this man.

Defiantly I said,

"I will not surrender."

Again, he smiled; his men stirred impatiently.

"No, I do not ask you to surrender. I ask you to be my guest. Here, please have some water as you must be very thirsty."

With that he offered me a flask that he had taken from his hip. Despite being parched I resisted and smiling, he took the top from the flask and sipped the contents before offering the flask to me again. This time I took it, and before I knew it, I had drunk all the water inside. This time I smiled as I returned the flask.

"Thank you but why are you doing this? Why do you want to save me from certain death? Especially as I have killed so many of your men."

"Allah is merciful and wants us to be merciful as well."

"I do not believe in Allah!" I snorted.

"No, but I do. Now please look around you. My men are not as generous as me. They want to kill you. You can stay here if you wish, or you can ride away under my protection. It is up to you. You choose."

As he said these words the tiny crack in my wall of indulgent self-importance began to split wider and allow reality to break through. I did not want to die a failure, a person who had wasted his life. Always I had been used to winning, to overcoming others with my skills and strength of will. I had believed I would die a glorious death with my heroism witnessed and retold in the tales of great heroes, forever remembered in legend. However, unless I chose to accept this enemy's offer, I would be doomed to die unnoticed and forgotten. Then, like a ray of sunshine penetrating the clouds after a storm, I knew I could not let it end like that. I realised that it was better to carry on living and perhaps get a second chance to make something of my life. Something in my demeanour must have shown I had accepted his offer because he turned and shouted some orders and one of his men brought his horse to him. Climbing up on his horse, he held out his arm which I grasped, and with his help, I swung up behind him. Then, and I do not really know why, I leapt down again and strode over to my shield which had been lying on the ground, picked it up and drove its point into the ground. Looking back, I think I just wanted to leave a mark. Having waited for me to climb back behind him my unexpected saviour rode away from his men leaving them bemused and angry. At this point my mind seemed to unravel. It was as if by the act of admitting that I had wasted my life I had released a dam and a lifetime of memories flooded every part of my consciousness. I began having extremely vivid dreams. One moment I was back in Wiltshur as a small child watching the men of the village arming themselves ready to fight the Vikings and being angry that I was not able to go with them. Then I was in Normandy discussing dowry terms with my future father-in-law, Sir Hugh de Beauville, as my future brother-in-law ranted and raved his displeasure, while Beatrice my future wife, sat silently and passively stared out of the window. Next, I was holding you, Aelfgar, my new-born son in my arms and weeping like a child. More and more memories flashed through my mind and with each one I was reliving my past. I think I must have passed out because I have no recollection of our journey. The next thing I knew I was lying on a bed in a luxurious palace. I later found out that my saviour was Prince Nazim of Aleppo.

As I sat there thinking back on those moments when my world collapsed around me, I felt proud of the progress that I had made since that time.

A few days later I was just finishing a breakfast of fresh fruit when one of the Palace guards came and found me, making it clear that the Emir wanted to see me. I must admit to being curious as to why the Emir wanted to see me now, as apart from the initial welcome I had not seen or heard from him. Unfortunately, the guard only spoke Arabic, so I had to be patient. As I entered the room, I saw the Emir seated at a low table and already seated around the table were Princess A'isha and Lady Elouise, both of whom I had also not seen since that first day. The Emir immediately came over and standing before me he touched his hand to his forehead and bowed his head slightly in my direction. He then gestured to an empty stool at the low table opposite his seat. Both Princess A'isha and Lady Elouise watched me as I approached and had welcoming smiles on their faces. Once I had sat down at the table the Emir returned to his seat and began to speak in Arabic. Princess A'isha began to translate his words.

"I hope you are finding your stay with us comfortable." I replied that I was.

"Dear Aethelwulf, please forgive the formality of this meeting but I wish to ask a favour of you and such things should not be done casually." He paused whilst the Princess finished translating before he continued.

"I have long been a believer that Allah moves in mysterious ways and it is sometimes impossible for us to understand his meaning or purpose." Again, he paused.

"I have had a problem for a while now that I have not been able to solve. The Lady Elouise is my guest and as such I am responsible for her well-being. Whilst the Lady is happy here and is very welcome to stay, she quite naturally wishes to fulfil her plans and continue to Italy to join her future husband and have a life with him. Now the problem is this; her future husband and her father will by now believe that she is either dead or in the hands of pirates. They are unaware that she is safe here with us. I could provide the Lady with a passage on one of my ships but what would she do by herself on her unexpected arrival in Italy. Alone and unprotected she would be at risk of abduction or worse. I could go myself to provide protection but, as I am a Muslim, I would not be welcome and would be in danger myself. There is the added complication that her future husband may no longer be awaiting her arrival and would need to be tracked down. I have pondered this challenging problem and have concluded that the ideal solution would be to have someone we could trust go to Italy on our behalf, find the Lady's future husband and arrange for him to come here to Tunis to collect her. However hard I tried, though, I could not think of anyone who could accomplish this on our behalf and this is where Allah intervened; suddenly you arrived from Aleppo. You have the presence of someone who could represent me in this matter and be of great service to Lady Elouise. Dear Aethelwulf, please would you consider travelling to Italy to find the future husband of Lady Elouise and arrange for him to come here and be reunited with his bride-to-be?"

When Princess A'isha had finished translating, I looked across at the Lady Elouise who sat smiling in my direction. I then turned towards the Princess who was doing the same, so I returned my gaze to the Emir. He was looking impassive, showing nothing of his feelings. They were all waiting for my reply. Inside my head there was a conversation taking place centred around whether I was ready to take such a step. One side of me wanted to repay the Emir for his hospitality and kindness as well as to be of service to the Lady Elouise, who had shown me such support and guidance earlier in the week. Of course, this new vulnerable me wanted to be well thought of by the Princess, who would be delighted if I accepted. On the other hand, I was anxious that I could not fulfil this mission successfully or, worse still, being forced to return to my arrogant, overbearing ways to successfully do so. As I sat there, conscious of their eyes upon me, I thought back to the last words of advice that Prince Nazim had given to me. I also thought of Lady Elouise likening me to the tiger trapped in an open cage by its fear of the unknown. Then quietly, without any fuss, I heard my gentler side say, as it had once before "You know what you must do."

I stood up from the table and, bowing my head in the direction of the Emir, I replied to his request.

"Your Excellency, it would be my privilege to go to Italy and do as you ask."

May 1069 Reggio Calabria

Three weeks later I was on one of the Emir's ships approaching the port of Reggio Calabria in Southern Italy. I was dressed as a Norman mercenary. This was the Emir's idea, he suggested that it might be wise to draw as little attention to myself as possible until I could discover the whereabouts of Lady Elouise's husband-to-be. The Emir had in his possession some Norman clothing and armour that had been taken when his ships had captured a pirate ship. I had chosen one that was old and well-worn. The chainmail outer layer was dented in places and in need of a clean. Likewise, the helmet had a dent in it, probably from a sword-blow. I did, however, choose a good quality sword, one that I could rely on if I had a need to defend myself at any time.

As soon as I had disembarked, I was met by a small group of Norman soldiers at the quayside. They had wanted to know who

I was, where I had come from and what my business was in Reggio Calabria. I explained that my name was Stephen de Beauville, that I had come from Tunis and that I was seeking Sir Hugo de Granville. The leader of the group demanded to know why I wanted to find Sir Hugo de Granville. So, I told him that I had some news of Sir Hugo's missing bride-to-be. The Norman laughed and said he hoped that it was the news of her death, otherwise I would not be very welcome. I, of course, was very curious to know why and it turned out that Sir Hugo was now betrothed to Duke Robert de Hauteville's sister. As the De Hautevilles were a much more powerful and influential family than that of Lady Elouise, Sir Hugo was keen to forget all about the engagement made in Normandy years ago. Furthermore, I found out that Lady Elouise's father was being held by Sir Hugo as a prisoner because he had objected to this later betrothal on the grounds that his daughter might still be alive and therefore Sir Hugo was still bound by his earlier betrothal. Sir Hugo would welcome news of Lady Elouise's death as it would allow him to marry his new bride-to-be without reproach but equally, he would not welcome news that she was still alive and wanting to fulfil their mutual promises. The leader of soldiers asked me what my news was, but I refused to tell them as I was honour bound to tell Sir Hugo alone and in person. They reluctantly accepted this and told me that Sir Hugo was across the straits of Messina in Sicily as part of Duke Robert's invasion force that was preparing to attack the Arab held town of Palermo. This caused me a moment of worry; I had not considered the possibility that I may need to return to the place of my near demise.

On enquiring, I discovered that all boats and ships had been commandeered by Duke Robert and all places on these boats were reserved for his soldiers. It seemed that, if I wanted to get to Sir Hugo, I would have to enlist in the Duke Robert's army and to do that I needed to report to the castle nearby. I made my way to the castle which was easy to see as it dominated the town. As I approached carrying my bundle of belongings on my back, I could see a group of Norman soldiers standing by the entrance. They seemed to be waiting for something or somebody. As I got nearer, they all turned to watch me and individually seemed to be examining me from head to toe. One particularly tall soldier broke away from the group and strode towards me.

"Name?" he bellowed. I was pleased to find that instead of reacting as the Aethelwulf of old, who would have bridled at this Norman's disrespect, I calmly placed my bundle on the ground and smiled.

"I am Stephen of Beauville, and may I ask your name, Sir?" The soldier slowly walked around me, examining my chain mail and weapons.

"I am Drogo of Caen, I am Duke Robert's recruiting sergeant, where have you just come from?" I continued to smile and replied in a matter-of-fact manner.

"I have just arrived by ship from Ifriqiya on my way back from Aleppo. I heard that your master was recruiting soldiers for his campaign in Sicily." I decided not to mention my mission to find Lady Elouise's husband to be. The tall Norman stopped his circling of me and stood close, staring directly into my eyes. I held his stare and maintained my smile. Suddenly he seemed to come to a decision.

"You better join these other down and outs. We are awaiting my master's arrival and then we will see what you are all made of" he said with a chuckle. I stepped over to the waiting group of soldiers and gave them each a cursory glance. To a man, they looked to be on the poorer end of Norman military class and this suited me perfectly. Strangely, I found it comfortable to play the part of a humble soldier rather that of a heroic knight. I had not long joined the group when several fully armed horsemen rode out of the castle gate at full pace. Drogo stepped forward and waited as the leader of horsemen slowed his horse and approached Drogo, who proceeded to give the horseman a verbal report occasionally pointing to individuals in our group including me. Having listened intently, the horseman walked his horse in our direction. He studied us carefully as he approached and held each of our gazes in turn. My instinct told me that this was Duke Robert. Giving his horse a gentle kick they trotted directly over to me. My years of experience living in and around warriors told me that I was about to receive a challenge of some kind. I readied myself, focussing on maintaining my humble demeanour.

"You, what would you do if you had been unsaddled on the battlefield and you were a target for an approaching horseman?" he shouted. I stepped forward, stood to attention, and replied in a strong but calm voice.

"I would wait until the charging horseman arrived and then I would unseat him and steal his horse."

"Would you kill him?"

"Probably."

"I want you to follow me; leave your bundle where it is, this will not take long."

Then turning his horse, he walked it into the middle of the square. I followed as instructed. He then told me to remain where I was, and he rode over to the group of horsemen and gave some instructions to one of them. Immediately that horseman drew his sword and spurring his horse on, charged towards me. I waited. I could see he was right-handed and that he held his sword high to his right and in his left hand he held the reins of his horse. The horse looked young, and I sensed it was inexperienced. He was nearly on top of me, but I still held my ground and just as he readied his arm to swing down towards me, I leapt to my right side, grabbed the reins as I went and in one movement dropped to my knees. As I landed, I tugged hard on the reins, then I let go of the reins and immediately leapt to my feet. The horse, as I had intended, veered dramatically to its left and the rider, who had been swinging down with his sword on his right side, had no choice but to go flying through the air. He hit the ground with a violent thud. The horse came to a halt nearby and I quietly and calmly walked over to it and took its reins. I looked over to the fallen horseman who was slowly gaining consciousness, so I climbed up onto his horse and rode over to where he lay. I dismounted and left his horse standing alongside him, I turned towards Duke Robert and bowed my head and in turn he nodded his approval. I returned to the spot where I had left my belongings. Over the next two hours each member of our group was selected and tested. At the end of that time four of us were still alive, two were dead and one was severely wounded. Once it was over the horsemen left and Drogo led us survivors into the castle. We were fed, given water and later shown to a dormitory where we were allocated a bed. A short while after, we were led to the armoury and issued with new armour and a sword, shield, and lance. We were then told to rest because tomorrow we would be crossing the Strait of Messina to Sicily. I took some time to take stock. I was pleased that my old warrior skills had not let me down, but even more pleasing was that I had passed my test in a way that fitted with my new self. I was now well and truly in the Norman world, as a common soldier and could now use the position to find Sir Hugo de Granville. Two days later, after what was a chaotic crossing, I found myself, along with thirty or forty other Norman knights, camped outside the walls of Messina. I was wondering how to go about finding Sir Hugo or in fact whether I really wanted to. If the information that I had received on arrival was correct, then I was in personal danger if Sir Hugo wanted to suppress the news that Lady Elouise was not only still alive but was keen to proceed with their betrothal. I also realised that by fulfilling my mission I would be putting Lady Elouise in danger as Sir Hugo could decide to permanently prevent her reappearance. I could just return to Tunis and inform Lady Elouise of the situation, but I could not ignore the fact that her father was held in prison by her unfaithful husband-to-be. My original plan had been to seek out Sir Hugo and hand him the letter I carried from Lady Elouise and await his response but now I needed a different plan. My thoughts were interrupted by the sound of my new name being called impatiently. I turned to see Drogo storming towards me. It turned out that he wanted me to join Duke Robert's personal escort in place of the soldier I had unhorsed during my recruitment test, who it seemed was still recovering in the infirmary. The good news was that Duke Robert was about to depart to join Sir Hugo outside Palermo, so I rushed to join his party. On the journey, I had no problem keeping myself to myself as everyone else seemed keen to do the same. As we approached the countryside around Palermo, we encountered regular checkpoints manned by Sir Hugo's soldiers. As we entered the main encampment we were met by Sir Hugo himself and his personal guard. Duke Robert climbed down from his horse and the two men embraced and greeted each other warmly. I remained at the rear of our party and tried to maintain a low profile but one of Sir Hugo's men stepped forward and whispered in his ear and to my horror pointed at me. In the same moment I recognised him as one of the men who had met me as I disembarked in Reggio Calabria. Sir Hugo then spoke to Duke Robert who summoned me to him. One minute I had been unnoticed and now I was the centre of attention. As I dismounted and stepped forward, I heard a quiet voice inside my head say, "Do not put Lady Elouise in danger."

It was Duke Robert who spoke, not to me, but to the man who had whispered in Sir Hugo's ear.

"Well man, is this the soldier you saw at the quayside?" The man replied nervously.

"Yes, your grace, this is the man, I am sure." Duke Robert turned his gaze towards me.

"This man here tells us that you have news of the fate of Lady Elouise. Is that right?" I briefly switched my attention to Sir Hugo, who looked perplexed and not at all happy. Returning my gaze to Duke Robert I replied.

"Yes, your grace, I have just arrived from Ifriqiya where I heard news of Lady Elouise from the Emir of Tunis. He had found out I was travelling to Italy and asked me to pass that news onto Sir Hugo and Lady Elouise's father, Sir Roger Fitzwarren, if I should meet them. On the sea journey I decided to use my initiative and actively seek them out and maybe find employment in their service."

Duke Robert and Sir Hugo exchanged glances. I could feel their unease but being soldiers who feared no-one they quickly came to an unspoken decision and Sir Hugo spoke directly to me.

"What is your name soldier?".

"I am Stephen de Beauville, Sir Hugo."

With that he put his arm around my shoulder and led me away from the group of soldiers including Duke Robert.

"Tell me what you have heard about the Lady Elouise." I took a deep breath and told him what he wanted to hear. I explained that the Emir of Tunis had a sizeable navy and that one of his ships had attacked and captured a pirate ship and in doing so had rescued Lady Elouise. However, Lady Elouise had been wounded in the attack on the pirate ship and had died a few weeks after her rescue. Before she had died, she had told the Emir that she had been on her way to Italy to join her father before marrying Sir Hugo. The Emir had promised her that he would get news of her fate to them both. Sir Hugo initially took the news well, in fact he looked pleased with it but then began to frown.

"How do I know that you are speaking truth and not just saying what you think I want to hear?" In answer I reached into my tunic pocket and retrieved the ring that Lady Elouise had taken from her finger as proof that I was representing her. I passed the ring to Sir Hugo.

"The Emir took this ring from the Lady Elouise's hand after she died and gave it to me, in case I needed to prove my story." Sir Hugo looked down at the ring, which he had given to his bride-to-be at their betrothal ceremony and studied it carefully before putting it in his pocket. He then put his arm around me again and led me back to the group and asked me to repeat my news to

173

the Duke. The Duke also seemed pleased at the news and muttered

"Good."

Later I lay in my tent thinking over the last few days and feeling confident for the first time that I had made the change to a new person. I was pleased that I had not reverted to my old self even once and I was beginning to feel certain that I could stop worrying that it would ever happen. My moment of reflection was ended by Drogo, who came storming into the tent I was sharing with three other soldiers. Drogo always seemed to be storming somewhere or other and, as always, he had no time for pleasantries.

"Sir Hugo wants to see you in his tent now. You had better get a move on, he does not like to be kept waiting."

When I arrived at this tent, the guard outside seemed to be expecting me and stood aside so I could enter through the open flap. Sir Hugo was seated at a table studying a map. He looked up and then turned in my direction.

"Ah, Stephen de Beauville, I need you to do something for me. I have spoken to Duke Robert, and he has agreed that I can use you to deal with a problem for me. Back in Reggio Calabria I have Lady Elouise's father, Sir Roger, held in the castle dungeon. He really is a nuisance of a man. He believes Lady Elouise may still be alive and insists that I delay my forthcoming wedding to Duke Robert's sister until we have definite news of his daughter's fate. He has been challenging me publicly to honour my vows and generally behaving annoyingly. So, I locked him up. He will not believe me if I tell him your news. Duke Robert has agreed that I can borrow you so that you may tell him on my behalf." Turning back to his desk he picked up a piece of parchment and signed it and then attached his seal. "This will get you through all my checkpoints and give you access to the castle dungeon. Here is the late Lady's ring, which you will, I am sure, need to convince the stubborn old fool that she is dead. When you have told him the news, I want you to suggest to him that he returns to

Normandy and stays there until he eventually dies in own bed. If he agrees to do this, give this set of instructions for his release to his guard. Otherwise, leave him there to rot." He passed me another piece of parchment with his seal on it and then abruptly turned his attention back to the map in front of him. It was at this point I cemented my transformation into the new person that I wanted to be. Instead of thinking of myself and what this assignment meant to me, I immediately thought of Lady Elouise and what it would mean to her. Clearly her betrothal to Sir Hugo was no longer viable and her priority would be to gain her father's freedom and for her and her father to be reunited. So, I remained where I was instead of leaving the tent. Sir Hugo looked up from his map and was visibly annoyed that I was still there.

"Well, what is it?" I chose my words carefully.

"I beg your pardon, Sir Hugo, but I have a suggestion that would get Sir Roger to leave Italy willingly." Sir Hugo put down his map and nodded for me to proceed. I suggested that I offer to take Lady Elouise's father to Tunis to visit his daughter's grave and meet the Emir as this would remove any doubt he may have about his daughter's death. Sir Hugo was pleased with this suggestion and provided me with further papers to provide myself and Sir Roger with safe passage to Tunis.

Three days later I was back in the castle in Reggio Calabria with Sir Roger who had been released into my custody. Two days after that we were aboard a trading boat entering the harbour in Tunis. I had felt it wise to keep up the story I had told Sir Hugo so that anyone overhearing our conversations would confirm the story. As we stepped off the boat we were met by the Emir's personal guard. It was at this point that I broke the news to Sir Roger that his daughter was alive and well and that he would be able to see her in a short while. Obviously, he was shocked by my news and suspicious of my motives and would not leave the quayside until I told him the whole story of his daughter's rescue and my mission on her behalf. In less than an hour he and Lady Elouise were walking arm in arm in the Emir's garden deep in conversation and with each of them amazed at the way things had turned out. I was at the same time giving the Emir a report on what had taken place; with Princess A'isha translating for both of us. I explained to the Emir what had happened during the time I had been away. He was curious about Sir Hugo and Duke Robert and their intentions and motives and whether I thought Tunis was under immediate threat from these Norman warlords. I told him in my opinion it would take them many more years to conqueror Sicily and then turn their attention elsewhere. After that meeting, Princess A'isha expressed her admiration for the way I had handled the situation and her pleasure at seeing me become confident in my new self. I was then visited by Lady Elouise and her father, both of whom wanted to thank me of rescuing Sir Roger and bringing them together again. I took great pleasure in seeing Lady Elouise so happy. I took this praise from everyone as evidence that I had changed significantly because it made me feel uncomfortable whereas before it would have made me swell with pride. I had indeed succeeded in making the changes that I had wanted to make but I still needed to find a way to dedicate the rest of my life to doing good for others and making amends for my past. The question was how? I remained in Tunis as a guest of the Emir while I pondered this question. One day, not long after my return to Tunis, Princess A'isha informed me that she had decided to return to Aleppo to open a new hospital there and to live with her brother, Prince Nazim, and that Lady Elouise was going to accompany her and she held out the opportunity of me joining them. Later, Lady Elouise came to see me. She explained that she saw herself in a similar place to me. Both of us were "dead" and therefore free to start a new life. She told me that her father, Sir Roger, had decided to return to Normandy to their family home and to see out his days there. He would maintain the story that his daughter had died in Tunis. So, she had decided to go with Princess A'isha to Aleppo and study medicine at the new hospital that was going to be built. She had already started to learn to speak Arabic from Princess A'isha. She also wondered whether I would be returning to Aleppo. I had thought about this after Princess

A'isha had mentioned it earlier, so I was able to answer Lady Elouise with some clarity.

"Part of me would love to return Aleppo to see Prince Nazim again and to spend more time with both Princess A'isha and you but my intuition tells me that I need keep moving onward and not go back to where I might be too comfortable. I have not found out yet what I mean by that, but I will, given time." She smiled and said that she understood and wished me well.

July 1070 Tunis

When the day came for them all to depart, I felt extremely sad. I was going to miss the Princess and the Lady. Their kindness and understanding had been pivotal in my resurrection. They had shown me, a stranger, such great kindness, and interest in my wellbeing. This experience had made me even more determined to find a path for the rest of my life that was focussed on other people's well-being. I watched as the ship carrying Princess A'isha and Lady Elouise sailed out to sea. Sir Roger had left a few days earlier. I had declined his offer to accompany him. The Emir had come to stand beside me as I watched. When the ship had disappeared around the headland, he suddenly turned to one of his guards and said something to him in Arabic. The guard stepped forward and bowing his head to the Emir and myself, started speaking.

"Sir, His Excellency has asked me to translate his words for him. Please forgive my poor Latin. I will do my best to convey His Excellency's words as accurately as I can. His Excellency has asked what you intend to do next. He says you are welcome to remain as his guest for as long as you like." I turned to see the Emir watching me intently with a warm smile on his face. I smiled back with genuine gratitude for his offer.

"Please tell His Excellently that I am not yet sure what I want to do next. I need to find a way to re-enter the world and in doing so find a way to be of benefit those who are in need of help."

After the guard has translated my words, the Emir spoke again and the guard nodded and turned to me. "His Excellency says he completely understands and repeats his offer for you to stay as his guest until you are able to see your way ahead."

So it was that I spent time wandering around the palace grounds contemplating my future and making little progress. One day the Emir appeared by himself and spoke to me in Arabic. I could not understand his words but there was no mistaking his tone of voice. It was kindly and supportive. After he had spoken, he took my hand and led me out of his palace and into the town. We were accompanied by four of his guards. After a short while, we stopped in front of a house. It was a plain house with white painted walls.

The front door of the house, however, was extremely decorative. It was painted in bright colours with the design of a tree. The Emir said something to one of the guards who then knocked loudly on the colourful door. After a short while the door was opened by a neatly dressed man who had a welcoming smile upon his face. The Emir said something to him, and the man stood back to let us enter. The Emir, smiling at me, held out his hand to indicate for me to enter first. So, I did and was surprised to turn and see the Emir and his men walking away towards the palace.

"Welcome Aethelwulf" said the man in perfect Latin.

"Please come this way". He then turned and went down a passageway into the house. I closed the door and followed. It is now clear to me that I must have trusted the Emir completely as I felt no qualms or unease in entering this house alone. The passageway opened out into a large bright courtyard and seated around a low table under a huge fig tree were two other men. As I approached them my host stood to one side and indicated for me to sit at the remaining seat at the table, which I did. As I took my place, I studied the three men in front of me. My host was the youngest of all of us. He was Arabic in appearance and he was neatly dressed in pale blue robes. Next to him was a much older man who had dark hair with grey streaks over his ears. From his dress I took him to be European. Finally, the third man was about my age and had a striking appearance with bright piercing green eyes and pronounced hooked nose. The one thing they had in common was that they were all smiling in a welcoming way. My host spoke.

"Aethelwulf, I must apologise for springing this surprise upon you, but the Emir was confident that you would not be offended by us doing things this way." I smiled back at these three men who obviously meant me no harm and told them that the Emir was right and the only feeling that I had at that moment was one of curiosity. My host began to explain that all three of them were members of an organisation called The Tree of Life and that the organisation's purpose was to come to the aid of people in need. He went on to explain that their society had been around for four hundred years and had been originally formed in Jerusalem to support pilgrims of all faiths on their journey to the holy land. Apparently, the founders of the society had laid down certain guiding principles that the society still followed. These principles were as follows: the society should be a secret society so that no member could gain a reputation for doing good and gain public and political benefit for doing so; the society should not be aligned to any organised religion but should be open to anyone who has a pure and generous heart who wanted to act only for the benefit of those in need. The founders also stipulated that to be accepted into the organisation, new members need to have demonstrated their purity of spirit and a desire to place the needs of others above their own needs. The founders had felt that unless this was done the organisation ran the risk of being usurped by individuals who would use the society for the own benefit and not for the benefit of others. They had seen this happen in their own religions and governments. My host told me that the Emir had identified me as a potential recruit for the organisation and had shared with the three of them the details of my rescue of Lady Elouise's father together with the circumstances and motivation of the rescue. He had also indicated to my host that I was actively seeking to find a new purpose for my life aligned to serving and bringing benefit to the needy. My host further explained that the Emir was also a member of the organisation. He had chosen not to be present at this meeting so that I would not feel obliged to accept their invitation to join them because I did not wish to offend. As he was telling me all this, I thought back to the time on the battlefield in Sicily when I realized that I was about to die an inglorious death and then was given an unexpected second chance. It felt to me that fate was intervening again to now give me a way to fulfil the remainder of my life. So, I agreed. I spent the rest of the day in their company, learning more details about the organisation, its history, rules, methods and finally the assignment they had in mind for me. It turned out that the man with the piercing eyes and hooked nose was Avhram ben Levi, who was about to return to Cordoba in Spain. I learnt that the civilised and open culture in the region around Cordoba, which had existed for centuries, was beginning to breakdown due to external forces pressing in on Cordoba. The Pope in Rome had issued indulgences that wiped out the sins of those who embarked on reconquest of Muslim-held Spain, which included Cordoba. Separately the Caliphate that governed Cordoba and was originally Arabic was being replaced by Berbers from North Africa. These new rulers, unlike their predecessors, were intolerant of other religions, especially the Jewish religion. Finally, into the mix was the interstate skirmishes between the various Catholic northern Spanish kingdoms which had led to wandering bands of mercenaries who sometimes strayed as far as Cordoba to pillage. The Tree of Life organisation wanted Avhram to extend their existing presence in Cordoba and organise safe havens and escape routes ready for the inevitable deterioration of law and order that was coming. Avhram felt I could be of great help to him and could contribute significantly to the future saving of lives. I agreed immediately and consequently we were shortly to be departing for Cordoba.

This was the last entry in his father's journal. Aelfgar rolled it back up again and tied it with the same banner that he had made all those years ago. He stared ahead at the Tree of Life design on the wall opposite and immediately thought of Rhiannon and how she had shared her beliefs with him. It occurred to him that if the world worked the way the Rhiannon had described on their journey to Escanceaster then his father's spirit that was now being recycled would be his new humble spirit, focussed on helping others. This thought gave Aelfgar some comfort.

Stevie put down the book and thought about the fact, that though it was not to the same extreme, her pre-rescue self was a similar person to how Aethelwulf had been in his early days. She took comfort in the way with the help of generous strangers he had been able to change.

Now that she had reached this point in the book, she understood why Joan Spencer had been determined for her to recognise the full scope of the Tree of Life's activities and not see it as just a hostage rescue organisation. She returned to the book as she was impatient to find out what Aelfgar did next.

Chapter 8

Strengths and Weaknesses

It was now two days since Aelfgar had finished reading his father's journal. He was still trying to absorb all that he had learnt, let alone make sense of all that had happened. His initial emotions were obviously sadness and anger at losing his father in the way that he did but also pride in how his father had changed his life for the better. Also, he felt gratitude for the fact that his father had provided the opportunity for him to learn from his father's life. Underneath these feelings was a background mood of amazement, that he had, despite all the odds, been able to find his father. It could be said that it was just a series of co-incidences that led him to his father's side, but Aelfgar felt there was more to it than that. Even though, to please his mother, he had attended mass regularly in Maeldubesburg, he had never felt any connection to God. He did however feel open to the spiritual ideas that Rhiannon and Ffraid both believed in. He was lost in his thoughts when it occurred to him that both he and his father had been on their own journeys that had led to this point. Sadly, his father's journey had ended but his own would go on. Where to next? At no time since leaving Maeldubesburg had he given any thought about what he would do if he succeeded in finding his father or, indeed, if he failed to do so. He recalled that when he started his journey his purpose was to get away from his uncle. It was Brother Dominic's dying words that led to his searching for his father. It suddenly struck Aelfgar that when he sat alone high on the tower above Maeldubesburg and made the decision to run away, he had no idea of the existence of the various people who would help him to find his way. There was Father Dominic, Ffraid, Aunt Aemma, Rhiannon and her brothers, the monks from Llandaff, the white-haired man from Escanceaster, the ship's captain and finally Mordecai and

Avhram. All of whom had nothing personal to gain from helping Aelfgar find his way but did so anyway. Aelfgar then thought about the various people who had helped his father once he dropped his self-righteous approach to the world. Prince Nazim, his sister Princess A'isha, Lady Elouise, the Emir of Tunis and the Tree of Life members in Tunis including Avhram. Again, none had anything to gain by helping Aethelwulf but did so anyway. He then thought about what he had learnt from the experiences he had on his journey. Certainly, he was more confident; he had learnt that there was a lot more to the world than life in Maeldubesburg and more satisfaction from giving rather than taking.

Mordecai and Avhram had discreetly kept their distance allowing him to deal with his loss in private but now Aelfgar felt the need for their company and advice. He wandered into the house and found them sat at a table studying some paperwork laid out before them.

"Ah Aelfgar my boy, how are you feeling today?" asked Avhram. Aelfgar smiled warmly at his host.

"I am well, thank you. I have been thinking about the last time I saw my father when he left Maeldubesburg. The person he was then and the person I saw briefly here were two different people and that in a way the father I knew did in fact die in Sicily and was born again in Aleppo. I am so grateful that, thanks to his journal, I now know what happened to him after he left that last time. More importantly, I know and understand why he never came back. I think I would have had more in common with the new father than the old. I have never really wanted to be a hero like he was. I have always been more comfortable helping others and being part of a group. I seem to be coming to the conclusion that I need to find a way to become the same kind of man that my father was trying to become." Mordecai and Avhram nodded in unison and Avhram asked.

"That sounds like great progress. Have you had any thoughts on how to go about that?"

"Not really, I seem to be bouncing between whether I should stay here and work on my father's plans with you or perhaps go to Aleppo and thank Prince Nazim, Princess A'isha, and Lady Elouise for helping my father; or whether I should return to live with my grandmother and aunt and perhaps Rhiannon; or even return to my uncle in Maeldubesburg and find a way to combat his wrongdoing. Having set my mind on finding my father, I never gave any thought as to what I might do afterwards. But now I know that I need to find a purpose I can be proud of."

Mordecai and Avhram both wanted to be of help to Aelfgar and decided to intervene. Avhram spoke first.

"Aelfgar, it is admirable that you want fulfil Aethelwulf's plans but each of us must find our own way to contribute to the wellbeing of others. Those plans were your father's and were for him to fulfil not you. He set them to redeem his soul before he died, but in the end, he did that by giving his life to save yours. He died with his plan made obsolete and with the joy of seeing you one more time as a reward. As far as Prince Nazim, Princess Aisha and Lady Elouise are concerned, they do not require any thanks. The best thing you can do is to assist someone else who desperately needs your help like you needed theirs."

Before Aelfgar could respond Mordecai spoke.

"Aelfgar, of course it would be natural for you to return and make your home with your grandmother and aunt. However, for you to be satisfied with that decision you need to be sure that it provides you with the best environment to give a lifetime of help to those who need it. The same goes for returning to your Uncle Ralf."

Aelfgar nodded and thought to himself

"Yes, I need to find something worthwhile to do with the rest of my life so that when I die, I will feel that I have made a positive difference to those in need"

London March 2017

As Stevie reached the bottom of the page, she saw the words "The End". She had both dreaded and paradoxically desired reaching this point. She closed her eyes and sat quietly for a while. She thought to herself that Aelfgar's last words could easily be her own. Then she thought about Chris and how this is what he would have thought when he had come to the end. She recalled him telling her that the book was written as a deliberate planned step in a recruitment process. He had said its purpose was to engage his attention with the idea of dedicating his life to helping others and to test his motives before he moved to the next step. Stevie opened her eyes and turned the page and found that she had not if fact finished the book for in front of her was a page entitled Epilogue. She began reading again.

Glean Da Locha April 1087

Aelfgar and Rhiannon stood silently by the gate of their fortified homestead. They were awaiting the return of their eldest son and another party of Anglo-Saxon fugitives. They had been living here in the centre of Ireland for nearly fifteen years. Their dwelling was positioned high on a hill and before them was a valley that at this time of year and this hour of the day, was filled with fog. As they watched, a group of riders and a covered wagon appeared out of the mist. One of the riders broke away from the group and galloped up towards them. It was Callwen their son. He leapt from his horse and gave his mother and then his father a big hug each. He then confirmed that the journey from Wexford had gone well with no problems. They all turned and watched as the wagon and accompanying horsemen reached the gate. One of the horsemen dismounted and nodding to Aelfgar he came and stood behind Rhiannon. It had taken a long time for Aelfgar to get used to the idea that, while he was away, Odo, his uncle's henchman, had been converted by Rhiannon into a loyal and trustworthy bodyguard. Rhiannon had told Aelfgar that, when she returned to Llandaff after leaving him on the outskirts of Escanceaster, she had found Odo sitting by the harbourside looking lost and defeated. She had taken pity on him and with her natural openness and authority she had persuaded him to return with her and her brothers and to stay with them. In a short time, Odo had become dependent upon her and her orders and seemed to completely forget his previous life with Lord Ralf. When Aelfgar returned Odo was no longer carrying a grudge and treated Aelfgar with the same deference that he showed Rhiannon. Over the following years he had married and had two children and was now a valued member of the community.

Beorhtric Eadgarson sat on his horse and surveyed the scene before him. His wife and daughter were being helped down from the wagon and then led to a roundhouse inside the enclosure. His son, Uhtric was steadying the horses and like Beorhtric, he was looking around him. The position of the homestead was well chosen.

As Beorhtric studied his new surroundings, he thought about how much had changed in such a short time. One month ago, he was one of the few remaining Anglo-Saxon lords in Angland who still owned his manor house and lands. He had known, since the arrival of William the Bastard that he was likely to lose it all but for twenty years that had not happened. Givelcestre, where his home is located, is deep in the county of Sumersaete and had gone unnoticed until the great survey carried out last year. When King William died, William Rufus his third son became King of Angland whilst his elder brother Robert became King of Normandy. As King, William Rufus wanted to reward those who had supported his claim to the throne. One of these individuals was William de Moyon, whom the new King made Sheriff of Sumersaete. William de Moyon was an extremely ambitious man and began building a motte and bailey castle in Dunster to enable him to control his newly acquired realm. In addition, he began forcibly taking possession of any manor and lands that the great survey showed was still in the hands of an Anglo-Saxon. So it was that William de Moyon arrived with a small army and forcibly evicted Beorhtric and his family from their manor house. He gave them until sunset to leave Givelcestre forever or face being slaughtered. Uhtric had wanted to put up a fight, but Beorhtric managed to persuade him to accept the situation and to leave without any resistance. Beorhtric and his family had no choice but to walk into the town of Givelcestre and seek help to escape. There they were helped by the townspeople to get to Wells Abbey Church where they were made welcome by the monks. However, whilst they were now clear of Givelcestre they were still in Sumersaete and the realm of William de Moyon. The Abbot felt it was best that they kept moving and he organised for the family to be taken by cart to Watchet and then by boat to Llandaff. They were able to rest with a family before crossing Wales to St Davids on the western coast. There, they were far from the reach of Willian de Moyon and any other Norman. Within a week they were once more on a boat, this time headed across the Irish sea to Wexford and there they were met by Callwen and brought to the place where he now found himself. He was still lost in his thoughts when Aelfgar approached him.

"Hail, Beorhtric Eadgarson, I am Aelfgar Aethelwulfson. Welcome to our homestead. We have prepared a roundhouse for you and your family. Please make it your home until you decide what you want to do with your future. You are our guests for as long as you choose."

Beorhtric studied Aelfgar intensely and saw only kindness and generosity in his face and in his demeanour.

"Hail, Aelfgar, thank you for your welcome. As you might expect I am still trying to adjust my mind to our rapid change in circumstances. Before I accept your generous offer, I feel duty bound to tell you that I have no means of repaying you for your kind charity. I was forced to leave behind everything I own when I fled Givelcestre."

Aelfgar placed his hand on Beorhtric's shoulder.

"No repayment is necessary now or anytime in the future. Come let us get you and your family settled."

Later that evening it was Aelfgar's turn to reflect on the past. On his return from Cordoba, he had travelled directly to Llandaff to be reunited with Rhiannon, Ffraid and his Aunt Aemma. He had avoided Maeldubesburg and his Uncle Ralf, who he had heard was in poor health and whilst physically weakened, it seemed that his bitterness and viciousness had strengthened as he tried to cling on to his power. Aelfgar had no desire to see his uncle again let alone confront him. Instead, he had dedicated his time and energy to creating an underground organisation with the purpose of helping those Anglo-Saxons who needed to escape the oppression of the Normans. So far, the number of families that he and Rhiannon had helped was in the hundreds.

A few years after his return he had travelled back to Cordoba and had been reunited with Avhram and Mordecai and had been given some of Mordecai's gold coins with which to help resettle his Anglo-Saxon refugees. Aelfgar thought of Aethelwulf and knew his father would have been proud of him.

Stevie had now finally finished the book and sat quietly for a while reflecting on Aelfgar's story. As she was about to close the book, she noticed a handwritten note inside the back cover. It said that when the reader had finished reading the book for them to ring the following number to arrange its return, just as Chris had described. This connection to Chris made her feel sad knowing, as she did, the consequence of his following this instruction. She decided to leave it a while before calling the number. She needed to get her thoughts straight before talking to anyone. She would sleep on it and then call her dad in Washington the next day to talk it over with him. She sent him a quick text to check when would be a good time for him and got an immediate reply. As she began to drift off to sleep, she tried to think of who in the world most needed help. When she awoke in the morning, she still had no idea. It seemed that the more she thought about it, the more people needing help popped into her mind. She started researching charities and good causes and the list of organisations was overwhelming. By the time it came to ring her dad, she was no clearer about what she could do to be of value to others. She got through immediately and her dad picked up on her weariness straight away. She explained her struggle and asked for help herself. George McMaster took his daughter's request seriously and stopped for the moment being the Secretary of State for the most powerful nation in the world and focussed on being Stevie McMaster's Dad.

"Two things spring to mind straight away, Stevie. The first is that there is no way that you can choose who to help in a rational way. How can you compare the needs of starving children in Africa with the needs of flood victims in South America or with the needs of victims of torture in Libya? It is not at all possible. Secondly, as a person you have a set of strengths and weaknesses and whatever you choose to do should make use of your strengths and not your weaknesses. So, let us start there and discuss what your strengths are and then we can see who might need someone with those strengths. How does that sound?"

"OK Dad, but I don't think that I have any strengths, only weaknesses."

"Yes, we all feel like that but ask yourself, how did I graduate with honours from Harvard University in Political Economy and Government. Clearly you have intelligence, work ethic, the ability to absorb complicated technical information. To be able to analyse it and form an opinion based on that analysis and be able to present your findings effectively to others. Those, for a start, are some good strengths. What did your tutors say about you in your academic reviews?"

Stevie switched her mind back to her university days. One of the things her tutors said about her was that she had a fiery passion for uncovering the truth, even if it meant hours of hard diligent work to do so. The other thing they consistently said was that she had the ability to present her research in a compelling and convincing way. Outside her studies, she often chose questionable causes to support. This often led to many clashes with the university authorities and often with her father. She would lecture him from a position of righteous indignation on matters like the invasion of Iraq and other, in her opinion, imperialistic policies.

"Dad, on the plus side they praised my research and presentation skills but on the negative side they criticised my rebellious anti-establishment outbursts."

"Yes, I remember that period. You were a rebel without a cause. Always challenging everyone's opinion; especially mine."

"And you were a distant and aloof parent that did not want to understand my point of view."

"Yes, Stevie, that was a difficult time for both of us. We really needed your mother around at that time to bash our heads together and make us see sense."

"Dad, I have been thinking about Mum's death lately. We have never really discussed its effect on us both. I was intending to raise it with you when I got back home, now that we seem to be getting on a lot better these days."

"Yes Stevie, you are right. We were both changed by her death. I lost my best friend my soul mate, and you lost your mentor. As I think about it now, I am ashamed of the way I buried myself in my work and neglected you and your needs. You became very rebellious because of my abandoning you. I am sorry Stevie. Please forgive me."

"That is ok Dad, as you say it was a difficult time for both of us. Let us continue this when I get back. Dad what kind of person was I when I was growing up?"

"Huh, the first thoughts that pop into my mind are that you were mischievous, fun loving and always curious. You always wanted to know how things worked. You could be quite obstinate if you thought you were right. You were a very friendly open child and were able to charm anyone if you wanted to."

"Dad, I am not sure this is working, I still cannot see what it is that I can do to help others. There are so many different people who need help and I cannot see how to choose any one of them over the others or what it is I can do that is practical."

"Stevie, have you heard the story of the boy and the starfish by Loren Eiseley?"

"No Dad, why?"

"Because it might help you see your problem from a different point of view."

"OK Dad, why don't you tell me the story."

"One day, an old man was walking along the beach in the early morning and noticed the tide had washed thousands of starfish up on to the shore. Up ahead in the distance he spotted a boy who appeared to be gathering up the starfish, and one by one tossing them back into the ocean.

He approached the boy and asked him why he spent so much energy doing what seemed to be a waste of time.

The boy replied,

"If these starfish are left out here like this they will bake in the sun and by this afternoon they will all be dead."

The old man gazed out as far as he could see and responded.

"There must be hundreds of miles of beach and thousands of starfish and you cannot possibly rescue all of them. What difference is throwing a few back going to make anyway?"

The boy then held up the starfish he had in his hand and replied,

"It's going to make a lot of difference to this one!"

"Dad, how does that story relate to me?"

"Well, to me it says just start with the first opportunity you get to help someone and then when they have benefited, find another opportunity and so on. There are so many people who need assistance; don't waste time trying to find the one with the most need, just serve the person nearest to you. Immediately Stevie's mind leapt to Aethelwulf's journal, which was still fresh in her mind, and Prince Nazim's advice in Aleppo to Aethelwulf and how Aethelwulf had started by carrying a basket for an old lady. "You are right Dad, but where do I find my first starfish?"

"I would say, stop thinking about yourself and what you want and open your mind and listen for a cry for help from someone in need. Let fate play a role in your quest."

Stevie thought about this. She certainly could not see a rational way to choose where to focus her time and she agreed that she could be helping someone right now instead of sitting in her father's flat in central London.

"You are right Dad. I need to get out and about and see what or who comes to my attention."

"Great Stevie, let me know how you get on."

"I will Dad. Thanks for your help. I feel better about things now. Bye Dad, I love you."

"I love you too Stevie."

Chapter 9

Finding the Right Path

London March 2017

Stevie then called the number in the book and arranged to return it. So it was that a few days later, she was sitting on a bench on the Embankment, staring at the Thames, lost in thought, when a voice next to her said

"Hello Stevie, it is good to see you again." Stevie gave a start. She had not noticed that Joan Spencer had sat down next to her. Stevie turned and thought that Joan Spencer looked less fierce this time; in fact she looked warm and friendly.

"It is good to see you again too. Thank you for lending me this book. It has got me thinking deeply about what I want to do next. It also made me think about Chris reading it and how it would have led to his coming to save me. You were right, I am not Chris. I must find my own way of helping others."

"I am glad you have been able to recognise that. What else has the book made you think about?"

"It helped me see that I have been like Aelfgar at the start of his story. I was alone and feeling confused and that I have been running away from something rather than towards something. Also, like Aethelwulf, I have spent my life up until now concerned solely with myself and what I want. An example would be that I hated my dad for not being there for me after Mum died but it never occurred to me that he was hurting as well and needed me to be there for him. I really like the concept of the Tree of Life and the one thing that will stay with me for the rest of my life is the idea that all of humanity is connected. I have not yet thought it through completely but the idea of us all being leaves on the same tree appeals to me."

Stevie took the book from her bag and passed it over to Joan, who in turn placed it in her bag.

"What are you going to do now?" Joan asked.

"To be honest, I do not know. I do want to have a positive purpose to my life and that means finding a way to help others but just now I have not found what that might be."

Joan stood up.

"Stevie, the Tree of Life organisation has never accepted individuals into its ranks without first witnessing an example of selfless altruism. As you have not yet carried out such an act, let us stay in touch and see where your search leads you and then maybe, we will be able to invite you to join us."

Stevie decided not to go straight back to her father's apartment, so she turned North and found herself in Fleet Street walking towards the Strand and Trafalgar Square beyond. It was late morning on a Sunday so most of the shops were closed. As she passed a travel agent's shop, she noticed a man curled up in the doorway. He was covered in old blankets, flattened cardboard boxes and was surrounded by numerous plastic bags full of old newspapers. She was about to walk past when the man stirred and sat up. It was difficult to judge his age, but he was not a young man. He rubbed his eyes and looked straight at Stevie.

"Good morning, young lady. I thought for a moment that you were my maid bringing me my morning coffee." He then started laughing which soon turned into a coughing fit. His body shook as he coughed and became worse before subsiding. Stevie stepped forward into the doorway and asked,

"Are you ok?" He slowly brought his coughing under control.

"I am fine Luv. Don't worry about me, you just carry on, I'll be OK." He then started rummaging through his blankets, as if he was looking for something. Stevie remained where she was but after a while she decided to move on as the man continued to ignore her. Further down the road she passed a coffee shop which was open. On the spur of the moment Stevie decided to buy the man a coffee and a chocolate muffin. Returning to the doorway where she had left him, she found someone else there with the man. As she drew closer, she could see that it was a young woman about the same age as herself. The woman was wearing a yellow, fluorescent vest and had a badge hanging from a lanyard around her neck. She looked up as Stevie approached. She quickly assessed Stevie's intentions and moved to one side. The man looked up at Stevie and saw the coffee and cake in her hands. "Hello again, are those for me?"

Stevie nodded and handed him the coffee and then the cake. His hands shook as he took them, and he spilt some of the coffee in the process. Stevie dug deep in her pocket and offered him some of those little sachets of milk and sugar, but he shook his head, so she put them back. Stevie turned towards the young woman who smiled at Stevie.

"Thank you, that was really kind of you. I am Susan, a volunteer with Help the Homeless" and with that she showed Stevie her badge as proof. Just as she finished speaking, the man started coughing uncontrollably again and was spilling his coffee everywhere. Susan bent down and took the cup from his hand.

"Jonathan, I hope your pneumonia is not coming back. How have you been feeling?" The man could not stop coughing enough to answer her and it was obvious that he was in great pain each time he coughed. The woman looked towards Stevie and asked her to stay and keep an eye on Jonathan while she phoned for an ambulance. Stevie watched as Jonathan overcame his coughing. He seemed exhausted and in a great deal of distress and needed to lean back against the wall to remain upright. Stevie did not know what she should do or say to help him. Before she could find an answer, Susan returned.

"An ambulance is on its way. We need to get you checked out in case it is serious." She paused and then added.

"Jonathan, you cannot keep sleeping in doorways. Winter is coming and you will end up dying in this doorway." The man looked up at her.

"Who cares?" he said bitterly. Susan smiled, not an amused smile but a caring smile.

"Well, I do" and before she could stop herself Stevie added "and so do I."

Just then the ambulance arrived, and a paramedic came to the doorway and checked Jonathan's pulse and listened to his breathing. The outcome was that he was helped up onto his feet and into the ambulance. Susan decided to go with him, so suddenly Stevie was standing alone on the pavement and staring at the pile of blankets and boxes and bags that were the only evidence of what had just taken place. Later, when she got back to her father's apartment, she thought about the man called Jonathan and wondered how he was. Also, she wondered how he had ended up sleeping in a doorway. She was annoyed with herself for not getting the charity worker's phone number so the next day she decided to call the charity and see if she could track down Susan. She got through to someone who knew who Susan was and who promised to pass Stevie's number on to her. Later that morning Stevie's mobile rang; it was Susan.

"Thank you for calling me back, I don't know if you remember me, but I am the person who brought Jonathan a coffee yesterday when you had to call an ambulance and take him to hospital. I haven't been able to stop thinking about him and hoping he is ok."

"Ah yes, I am sorry to say that he is very unwell. As I had feared his pneumonia has returned and they have discovered that his liver and kidneys are in a bad way. The doctors were not expecting him to survive the night."

Stevie found herself surprisingly upset at this news.

"Poor man, I am so sorry. You must be sad. Have you known him long?"

Susan told her that she had personally started trying to help Jonathan just over a year ago but with little success. She also explained that it was quite common for her clients to die.

"The problem is that we get to them too late. They have usually been sleeping rough for a while and tend to be unwell, both physically and mentally. In addition, they are often resorting to drugs or alcohol to get through the day."

"But surely you are able to help some of them get back on their feet."

"Yes, some but not enough. The answer is to get to them when they first lose their home for whatever reason. Anyway, thank you for showing Jonathan a little kindness yesterday, he would have appreciated it. I am sorry but I must go now as I am on duty again in a minute."

Stevie sat for a while thinking about what Susan had said. She also found herself thinking about her earlier conversation with her father. Was homelessness the cause that she should focus on? Was it her nearest starfish? If it was, what skills and abilities did she have that could be used to help the homeless?

A few days later she was back in the café where she had bought the cup of coffee for Jonathan. She was listening intently to Susan, the charity worker, as she described Jonathan's descent into rough sleeping. Stevie had told her father about what had happened after their last phone call and in telling him about Jonathan she realised that she got a lot of energy and determination when she thought specifically about Jonathan rather than the generic problem of homelessness. As a result, she contacted Susan to find out more about Jonathan and how he ended up as he did.

"By the time they come to our notice their confidence and self-esteem are rock bottom; They seem unable to stop themselves spiralling downwards until, like Jonathan, their bodies give up. We try to help them but unfortunately, in most cases, it is not enough. We need as a society to change our approach to homeless people. We must turn things on their head. Currently we wait until people are sleeping in doorways before we step in as a society and help. Most people who walk past their doorway ignore them, though a few like you take pity on and show some kindness. We work with the local councils to try to help but the system, the way it is set up, presents the authorities with a series of barriers that they are not equipped to overcome."

"What do you mean?"

"Well, if you take Jonathan as an example. Five years ago, he was running his own business and employing fifteen people. The economy went into a slump. To cope with the pressure, he began drinking and within a year he was a secret alcoholic and losing grip on his life. The outcome was that his business went bust and his wife divorced him. He lost his house and could not find employment and ended up begging and sleeping rough. Over time his health deteriorated and understandably he became seriously depressed. My charity discovered him about two years ago and found him a place in a hostel and helped him to claim the benefits he was entitled to and get treatment for his alcohol addiction. However, his self-esteem was extremely low, and he was overwhelmed with guilt and self-loathing for his weakness and its consequences. Furthermore, he hated sharing his accommodation with others who were in a similar situation as they were a reminder of his own inadequacies. As soon as he had accumulated any money he would relapse, get drunk and return to sleeping in doorways. He seemed to believe it was what he deserved and was a kind of penance for his sins. After every period of rough sleeping and alcohol abuse, he would end up in hospital and we would be contacted to try again. As I said we were too late, we were helping him when he was at his lowest and least capable of lifting himself back up even with our help. In some countries like Finland, they have changed their response so now they intervene at the beginning when a person loses their home and they immediately provide them with a home and support to help them before their physical and mental health deteriorates. I wish we would do the same here." Stevie listened as Susan spoke and wondered why this was not happening. Then later she thought about her home country. How many people like Jonathan were there across the whole of the USA? She thought about all the other countries around the world. She began to feel the anger and indignation rise in her as it did when she was protesting as a student. This time instead of criticising others she felt it was up to her to change things but how to do that?

Chapter 10

Yes and I did

New York August 2022

As Stevie approached the podium, she allowed herself to recall the moment five years ago when she stood in that doorway in London watching Jonathan being taken away in an ambulance to die alone in hospital and then she allowed herself a moment to recall Chris's body collapsing upon her in the helicopter as she flew to freedom. By the time she had reached the lectern at the front of the podium her whole being was motivated and focussed on getting this diverse and influential audience to take the immediate and co-ordinated action that she was about to request from them. She had spent the last year working with a small team of helpers to identify those individuals in the New York area who had shown tangibly that they cared about their fellow man. They could be politicians, corporate executives, religious leaders, civil servants, charity workers, academics and others. What mattered equally to their caring for the needy was that they had shown they were prepared to act if they believed in a plan. The approach that Stevie was about to present had a three-pronged strategy. Firstly, there was the plan to build cross-organisational initiatives that connected existing initiatives to eradicate homelessness in Greater New York. Secondly, the plan to create a new way for businesses to benefit from providing active help to employees to transition from employment with them; be it redundancies, sacking, retirement or physical or mental health crises. Finally, there was the plan to provide incentives for housebuilders to provide sufficient levels of affordable accommodation to meet the need within the economy. It was her vision that no one would ever become homeless as they would be helped to keep or find a new home. Her basic message was about switching support from after the event to before the event. There are many reasons that people become homeless including becoming unemployed, domestic violence, substance abuse, being the victim of flood, drought or fire. Also, business failure, illness, and debt. Quite often a person can become homeless because of a combination of a number of these. Stevie believed that it would be much easier to help people to overcome these crises if they were in their own home and were able to live as normal a life as possible while being helped to recover from their misfortune.

Sitting in the audience was George McMaster, who was now retired from public life but had been working tirelessly alongside Stevie. As he sat there in the front row, it occurred to him that at some stage in every parent's life, if they are lucky, there will be a moment when they look at their child and realise that they are now well and truly their own person. This was George's moment. He thought of how proud his wife would have been to see Stevie stand before the great and the good of New York and hold them in the palm of her hand. What had really impressed George over the past five years was that whilst Stevie was building her strategy, identifying allies and overcoming resistance, she still found time to walk around the city and its suburbs and speak directly to the homeless people that she found. When she returned home from such an evening, she was always more energised and motivated than ever. For her, the homeless were not numbers on a chart but individuals who had dreams and fears and had just needed a helping hand. Not far from George McMaster in a seat a few rows back sat Joan Spencer. She was one of the many members of the Tree Of Life organisation who were scattered around in the audience. She and the organisation had been actively supporting Stevie to launch her initiative.

New York July 2090 CE

Stevie lay there drifting in and out of consciousness. Sometimes she was aware of people in the room and of the door opening and closing and at other times she was lost in fleeting memories from her long life. When she was conscious, she could feel her strength slowly draining from her. She had never been afraid of death, just of wasting her life. Right now, in her mind, she was back in the room in the mansion house when she had first approached the Tree of Life organisation seeking to join them as hostage negotiator way back when she was a still naïve but driven youngster. The bright-eyed and sharp-minded little Joan Spencer, who was interviewing her, was saying

"Stevie, I am concerned that picking up the baton from Chris Smith is not the right way for you to repay him for sacrificing his life to save yours. You are not Chris and will never be. I accept that you want to dedicate the rest of your life to helping others in need, but our assessment is that you are not cut out to be a hostage negotiator. There are many other ways to be of help. We all need to find our own way of making a difference for the good with the time that we are given. Can you find yours?"

Her daughter, who was sitting by her bedside, was surprised when her mother suddenly spoke out loud and then stopped breathing. Her daughter tried to replay her mother's last words in her head. She thought that it sounded like

"Yes, and I did".

New York Times Date 27/07/2090

We are sad to report the passing of Stephanie "Stevie" McMaster-Brown at age of 98 from natural causes yesterday at 3:35pm surrounded by her family. Stevie was the daughter of past Secretary of State George McMaster and Mrs Christine McMaster. Her husband, Ronald T. Brown sadly passed away earlier this year at the age of 93.

When she was a teenager Stevie was kidnapped by a terrorist group in Syria while driving an aid truck for the UN. She was subsequently rescued at the cost of her rescuer's life. This experience acted as a spur for Stevie to dedicate her life to helping others. She has been credited with being one of the major reasons that homelessness in and around New York, Washington DC, and many other major cities in the US has been entirely eradicated for decades.

Her funeral will be held in private at the local chapel near her home. She will have a simple gravestone with the words "We are all leaves on the same tree" inscribed on it. Her family have requested that no flowers be sent but instead have asked that mourners and those offering condolences plant a small tree in their garden and watch it grow.

Authors Notes

I started writing this book 15 years ago. I had not set out to write a book. I was just writing ideas down as they popped into my mind.

In the beginning I had been wondering why terrorists were willing to blow themselves up in public spaces with the intention of killing large numbers of people. It seemed to me to be completely wrong to have something so negative as a purpose in life. So I started thinking about an alternative. A story about individuals striving to do something positive with their lives by helping others.

I thought about how potential suicide bombers were recruited and groomed by terrorist organisations and what kind of organisation would be the positive equivalent. I thought about how, unlike terrorists, this group would not want to use a manipulative or coercive approach to engaging and encouraging a potential recruit.

The first step was to give some shape and identity to this group that was responsible for finding, directing and supporting these recruits. In the end I settled on calling it the Tree of Life organisation and the idea that every human being was like a leaf on the same tree. Much later I added a chapter that told the story of the origins of this organisation in the 7th century.

At some point I had the idea that a book containing a story about a young boy seeking a purpose to his life could be used within my story as a tool to open the mind of a recruit and test their interest in dedicating their life to helping others. Initially I considered setting this second story in a fictious world but eventually I decided on the story beginning in 11th century Malmesbury.

I am not a historian, and my level of research has not been as deep as experts in the subject would have gone. I have used history where I could, to colour and shape these stories but I have also invented some parts based on research. For instance, I could not find any reference to a castle in Malmesbury until the 12th century when a stone castle was built. However, I discovered that the Normans brought prefabricated wooden castles with them when they invaded in 1066CE. So I start this part of the story at the top of a wooden castle in 1070CE.

Along the way I have received a great deal of help from some generous friends and family to help me turn my rough-hewn version into a finished book. I would like to thank David Charles, Paul Deacon, Bill Reed and Geraldine for their invaluable help.

Chas Gould

31/10/2022